A CLAREWOMAN'S JOURNEY

by Anne Loughnane

Formatted for publication by WriterMotive
www.writermotive.com

Contents

Frontispiece

...... the life path of the individual may be our best portal into the actuality of the past and by extension the broader historical canvas. Everyone carries the imprint of other lives within their genes, like engendered ghosts whose near or distant dramas beckon from the dark within us and the limbo of lost record or witness. Historical record has tended to exclude or overlook women's lives in particular.

Michael Coady Irish Poet & Writer

Michael Coady is published by Gallery Press and is a member of Aosdana

CHAPTER 1

Encroaching Shadows 1974/75

I caught sight of the black and white collie out of the corner of my eye as I drove towards Doonbeg. He was coiled as if to spring, *the Lord save us* , I swerved violently to avoid impact as the collie leapt snarling at the little Morris Minor. Thankfully I hadn't hit him, and he was racing along beside me. Gradually he fell back, wagging his tail in satisfaction, clearly feeling that he had given me a run for my money. I parked at the entrance to a narrow green road just beyond the village and wiped the perspiration from my forehead. I was to discover that this kamikaze behaviour on the part of West Clare's collies was widespread and wondered if there was a genetic explanation. I set off as directed, down the lane, its hedges almost bare now, keeping me close, dripping company on that November day.

It had taken me a long time to find the place. In vain I strode up and down the boreen looking for any sign of human habitation. Returning to the village for directions, I had been firmly sent back to look again, and sure enough I spotted the run down cottage I'd initially taken for a ruin, a short field away. It looked scarcely habitable. There was a thin spiral of smoke emerging from the central part of what had been a three-roomed cottage. The rooms at either end had half fallen in and only a grassy thatch remained, sheltering the middle section. With no very defined path to guide me, I made my way across the field and knocked at the sagging door, noting the unsightly piles of rubbish beside it, before entering. I found myself staring at a ragged old woman who was struggling to rise, and from whose soot-begrimed face two shrewd grey eyes appraised me. She was small, dressed in a long dark skirt with what looked like a very dirty flannelette shirt and a man's pullover with holes in both sleeves. She welcomed me with real grace, however her well-spoken tone of voice belied the image she presented.

I had been in my job as West Clare's first professional social worker for a few months now, and my trusty Morris Minor was becoming very familiar with the network of little roads that criss-crossed the county, taking me to all sorts of villages that, as Flann O'Brien had it, "strictly speaking weren't on my way". The local council housing officer had urged a visit to eighty-five-year-old Eilin O'Brien and her son, in order to persuade the old woman to accept re-housing by the council. They described her circumstances as shocking and were clearly embarrassed to have one of their constituents living in such appalling conditions in the mid-Seventies.

> Eilin was surprised by the swish of footsteps through the wet grass. "Hello, hello Mrs O'Brien?" "Yes, yes." She levered herself out of the old car seat covered with worn clothes and a few old blankets. These had made a comfy nest for her these good few years now. She stared at the strange young woman, younger surely than Marie, the district nurse who dropped in now and then. "I'm Anne Loughnane, your local social worker …" She didn't rightly know what a social worker was, though she'd sometimes read in the paper about them. They seemed to be about children mostly, poor children who weren't looked after; sure there was a lot of cruelty in the world. She seemed sure of herself this young woman, but friendly too, without any shadows.

She didn't know why the harrowing images that had overshadowed her parents' lives had come to haunt her too as the years closed in God rest their souls, there had been little peace for them; "Wisha come into the fire 'tis cold outside," she said to the young woman.

I sat down fairly gingerly on the only remaining chair by the fire. It was a sorry affair with only two of the original four slats on the back remaining, and I hoped that I wouldn't finish it off. It was surprisingly cosy by the fire, despite the wind whistling through what were fairly alarming holes in the grassy thatch which sheltered them. I took off my coat and then was sorry as there was nowhere to hang it. I placed it awkwardly over my lap. Eilin didn't seem to notice and was busy pushing the ancient kettle back over the fire on an old iron fire-hook. I had only ever seen these in pictures, as even my Gran had a black, closed range which I remembered having to blacken with a kind of polish when I visited.

I looked around the dingy room, its only furniture some dilapidated chairs, a smallish square deal table and a rough cupboard with the door hanging off the hinges. This probably contained some delft and utensils. A picture of the Sacred Heart, slightly flushed by the little oil lamp glowing red underneath it, decorated one grimy wall. There was some comfort from the warmth of the turf fire, though the clouds of smoke shunted back into the room by the strong wind gusting down the chimney soon had my eyes streaming. There was a sliced white loaf spilling out of its bag and a full pound of butter, its wrapper slightly opened, with little troughs dug out of it, on the table. This, together with a dirty floral cup and an intact but stained white mug and some bits of used cutlery, was all that remained of their last meal. There were two doors leading off the kitchen at either end. These led into what Eilin called "the room above" (beyond the hearth wall) or "the room below" at the opposite end. Neither of these can have been water-proof judging by the state of the roof, but I was to learn that Eilin never let anyone into the room above, not even her son Sonny, and not until she died would I understand why.

During that first visit, I explained to Eilin that the County Council was keen to re-house her. It would be a nice new house with a bathroom, hot and cold running water and a lovely new kitchen. "Arra, amn't I fine as I am," Eilin said, and "how much would all that cost me anyway." "It would only be a tiny bit of your pension, and you'd not need to worry about repairs or anything, as the Council would be responsible for all that." Not, I thought, that she'd be worried about repairs by the look of this place. Eilin didn't seem very happy about this prospect and shifted uncomfortably. "Well," she confided, "I've heard tell of lots of folk who get free houses and I'll not go anywhere unless I get a free one too. You know child, it's all pull, the councillors look after their own, but sure it's not your fault, will you have a sup of tea now." At her ease again, she vigorously poked the fire, bringing it to a bright blaze.

I knew that she was probably referring to the houses erected as a result of the Labourers Cottage Act of 1880. A number of her neighbours, whose dwellings at the time had been in a deplorable state, had benefited from this. Clearly it would be difficult to get Eilin to accept that things were different now and that it wasn't about pull; such long memories, accompanied as they often were by deep distrust of the authorities, were a curse.

> Eilin sighed, sure the child, what did she know of hardship? Why was this cloud of anxiety enveloping her; would she become like her mother Annie whose whole life had been shrouded in a despairing mist? But then, things had been bad for her mother's family. It was her

mother's Aunt Cait and cousins who ended their days in Kilrush workhouse when her uncle Breandan died. Eilin's father, Paidi, remembered Breandan as a great cheery man who used to take him up in his cart when going to cut the turf in Tuohy's bog. Breandan would light his pipe and gaze out over the dark quiet scene telling him that it was a grand day for the bog, whatever the weather. Paidi loved to watch him slicing the sods of turf and could never work out how he managed to make each one identical in size, as he slung them up onto the bank without a bother. He recalled his great laugh when, as a little boy, he struggled to lift the sods, heavy with water, and Breandan would bend down to bolster his tiny arms with his own big strong ones.

Paidi described Aunt Cait as a comical creature who would dance and lilt at the drop of a hat, though she was fiery too and it's many the skelp he got for bringing muck into their cabin when she'd swept it clean. He'd often go up there after supper, and she'd teach them to dance a polka or maybe a reel while she lilted a tune. She had an old wheezy melodeon that she sometimes played, though he used to notice that there were a lot of notes missing. Everyone just had potatoes for supper then, sometimes with a drop of milk, or fish, when Breandan's brother, who was a fisherman in Kilkee, dropped by. The couple had five children, and their youngest, Mikey, could already pick out notes on the old melodeon and was a grand little singer too.

Eilin recalled her grandfather's description of the fear on Breandan's face that awful late summer day in 1846 when the putrid smell of decay was all around them. They had been so sure that they'd have a great crop that year, having worked hard to cover every yard of their little fields with seaweed, sand and manure. Brendan said that it seemed to come out of nowhere; the very same potato fields that were green and flourishing when he passed them on the way to the bog that morning, were now a dark soggy mass of corruption. They couldn't believe that it could happen so quickly. He bent to pick up one of the rotting stalks and feel underneath, but it was a wet sticky substance that came away in his hands.

Breandan didn't know how he was going to feed his family, as the pig they had would be needed to pay the rent. Failure to pay this would mean eviction from their home, and this was already happening with other poor souls. God is good, and at least they'd got enough sound seed potatoes to plant for the following year. God willing they'd get through the winter. He could pawn his frieze coat, and there was talk of public works being undertaken by the Board of Works. Well he was taken on by the Board of Works for eight pence a day, but this was not enough to feed Cait and the family, and they eked it out by pawning whatever they could.

Eilin's grandfather, Paidi Mor, was also taken on by the Board of Works, and he would never forget the icy Atlantic gales blasting over them as they toiled at making a new road from the west end of Kilkee, over that bleak coastline. They were weak with hunger all the time, but at least he d got his frieze jacket. Breandan had nothing but a worn old jacket given to him out of pity by the local parish priest. He succumbed to the fever the following February and died before they could even get him back to Cait, God rest him. The poor woman was distraught, with five little ones to feed and care for. "What am I going to do Paidi Mor?", she'd asked, and he felt the shame of not being able to do more than give her a share of the pitiable amount of the Indian meal they relied upon at the time. For a while during that year, they were able to drag on with help from some of the soup kitchens being set up, and Brendan's brother brought them the odd bit of fish, though the fishermen too were in a bad way. They didn't have the boats or equipment except for inshore fishing which yielded very little, and in fact, many of them had to pawn the poor equipment they did have, to put food in their family's mouths. He was able to get them some clothes through the Ladies Clothing society in Kilkee. It was the Quakers who gave them parcels of clothes for distribution to the poor. God be good to them, they fed them when they were starving and didn't be trying to convert them to their religion either.

Her grandfather told them that Aunt Cait and her five children were transformed into spectres before their eyes. They got scraps of food from the outdoor relief at the poor house in Kilrush, where Cait would drag herself the seven weary miles and back every week. Paidi Mor tried to encourage her to hang on, in the hope of a better harvest the following year. He had been able to save some seed potatoes to sow for her, as well as himself. "I don't know if we can last till then Paidi Mor," she told him. All the children were ill, and what they and the other neighbours had to give them, an old turnip or the odd bit of gruel, soon dried up. They'd been living on boiled nettles for weeks when they all got dysentery, and little Mikey became so thin and pale that he could hardly get up of a morning. Seamas, her eldest, trying at twelve to fill his father's shoes, went begging in Kilrush for scraps of food, "a thing I never thought could happen to our family," Cait said sadly. By then she was little more than a wraith herself.

Well, they dragged on and were heartened the following August, to see the potato plants they'd lavished such care on, sturdy and green. Surely this time the plants would flourish? Paidi Mor recalled the morning when a wail went up from all around the countryside; the blight had struck again. The stalks and lovely green leaves were just a brown soggy mess plastered over the fields. Poor Cait lost all hope when she had to bury Mikey's little body just wrapped in straw. She had to be stopped from putting her ragged old cloak around the straw, *to keep the worms from the little cratur for a while.* He had caught typhus fever which was very common at that time. The remaining family were taken by cart to the workhouse and fever hospital in Kilrush. They knew that they were going there to die, but sure at least, they had the comfort of knowing they'd get a coffin to lie in.

I was surprised by the vehemence of Eilin's response when I asked her if she was still troubled by the inherited memory of those harsh times. "Sure to be sure I am child; couldn't they easily come again?" and she poked the embers of the fire in some agitation. I reached over spontaneously to take her hand, "What a hard life you've had, Eilin." She stared at me then and seemed genuinely amazed, and I was astonished when she laughed. "Yerra child, indeed and I didn't, I had a great life sure we had great fun." She stared into the fire again a smile playing around the corners of her old lined mouth, clearly remembering …

Years later the words of Michael Coady's poem, *Time's Kiss* would call to mind that first encounter with Eilin…

> *OLD WOMAN*
> *The past is a wind*
> *that moans behind her,*
> *a draught around a door*
> *she can't keep closed.*

CHAPTER 2

Stories That Haunt

It was a wet afternoon, and I hadn't wanted to leave the glowing turf fire in my flat in Kilrush. The sitting room, where I'd spent the morning working on case notes, was nicely warmed up, and the thought of a second visit to that bleak abode was not appealing. My little flat was on the top floor of a two storied building overlooking the town square. It consisted of a small bedroom, an even tinier kitchen and a good sized sitting room with two windows looking onto the square. The bathroom was on the landing between the two floors, but I'd got used to this inconvenience. There was a shoe shop on the ground floor, and the stairway was always crammed with cardboard boxes. Friends asked if it was spooky being all alone in an empty building at night time, but I didn't feel lonely and loved to watch the goings-on in the square below. I glanced now around the low-ceilinged room admiring the vibrant greens and blues of the Avoca rug thrown over the old couch. I felt that the cheap prints of Picasso's *Mother and Child* and Van Gogh's *Starry Night* lent a whiff of urban sophistication to the room. "Oh well," I sighed and negotiating the shoe boxes, walked out to where I'd parked the Morris.

Crossing the square I was struck again by how substantial it was. It was well proportioned with solid buildings and a town hall which had replaced the old market hall at its centre. I knew that it had been a planned town developed by

Anne Loughnane

the local landlord family, the Vandeleurs, who in the latter half of the nineteenth century were to become infamous as evicting landlords. The astonishingly wide Frances Street connecting it with Merchant's Quay, and on around to Cappa Pier, bore witness to the town's history as a trading centre. From the early nineteenth century boats carrying corn, wheat, butter and turf plied regularly between Kilrush and Limerick. Though such trade was now long gone, I thought that the town retained a sense of grandeur, possibly because of its generous layout, and its dramatic location where the mighty waters of the Atlantic and the Shannon merged.

There was nothing grand about the twisting road through a sparse scrubby landscape that led me from Kilrush to Eilin's house just outside Doonbeg and more of the recollections that would fill my imagination over the coming months.

Eilin woke to find herself sandwiched between the wall and her sister Bride. The latter was lodged, as usual, in the deep hollow gouged out in the centre of the big double straw mattress they shared. It's a wonder I'm not squashed to smithereens between the wall and that great lump, she thought but didn't voice, having a healthy respect for her relatively fragile person. Then she remembered and squealed with joy, it was the first day of the summer holidays; no more school for … for… forever. Her brother Sean, who shared the other double mattress in the room, let out an answering yelp of exultation and thumped his brother Dan. "No more of the oul tyrants," he shouted. Dan pulled the bedclothes around him and turned to the wall. "Get up, get up you lazy oul boots," and Sean gave him another thump. Dan pushed him out of the bed: "Will you let me be and go drown yourself," he grumbled, but Sean was having none of it, and soon they were at it, hammer and tongs.

She slipped out during a lull in the melee, and keeping a wary eye out for her mother, who was feeding the hens, grabbed the jam jar she had left ready the night before. She raced down the hill under the bridge where she couldn't be seen from the house. With any luck, the henhouse would be cleaned out by the time she got back. She hated cleaning this dirty smelly outhouse; why were hens so filthy? Her mother made her take her turn, which would have been today, but maybe she'd forget. She hugged herself with delight as the mist began to clear and she noticed how the golden buttercups carpeting the opposite bank faded into the dark green of the firs beyond. Carefully laying her jam jar wedged where it was sure to catch minnows, she wandered upstream, hopping from one softly carpeted mossy stone to another and relishing the clear sparkling water. She was brought up short by the odd sharp pebble but loved the squishy mud wriggling up between her toes. She caught sight of the warm chestnut plumage of a chaffinch and noticed how the gorgeous fluorescent greens and blues of a dragonfly glittered when the sun caught them.

"Eilin ...Eilin," it was her friend Mary Moloney calling, "I'm here," she shouted, waving as she caught sight of her tousled red curls. "I'll race you," cried Mary, to see which of them could jump the stream at its widest. She grumbled, "Why do you always have to be racing?" Choosing their spot they ran to give them a good spring from the bank, and what a great feeling it was to collapse safely on the other side. Sean, who was a right harum-scarum, arrived not long after. He was tall and lanky with a mop of spiky black hair and was like a dancer at the leaping. He'd take a run of thirty yards or so, slow at first, but building up speed until he thrust himself into the air to sail over the widest part of the stream. She heard her mother calling then. "It's the oul henhouse for me," she told Mary, who helped her with it, and sure they made light work of it together. Those summer days seemed long and sunny, trawling with Mary along the edges of meadows, threading wild strawberries through long grassy stalks, or swimming with Sean and Dan in the millrace behind Ryan's mill. It was dangerous racing across the slanting roof of the mill, and leaping in to where the water gathered deeply before surging over the vertical fall to the narrow stone channel below, but she loved the thrill of it. They were quick to demolish the huge pile of steaming potatoes with the hunger that was on them when evening came. Sometimes they'd get burnt throwing them from one hand to the other to cool them, and she loved to lick the butter from her fingers when it ran down the side. Potatoes, with their jackets split open and a dollop of butter, and maybe a bit of bacon or fish sometimes, washed down with big mugs of buttermilk, was what they had for dinner most evenings.

Eilin looked up suddenly at the sound of the door being pushed open, "is that you Sonny," she called out. "It is Mammy." A pale round-faced man in early middle age wheeling a heavy old-fashioned bicycle stared at me, dumb-struck. "D'ye see the fine young woman I've got for you now." "This is my son," she added for my benefit, her old eyes alight with mischief. Poor Sonny didn't know where to look and seemed very ill at ease as I stood up to shake hands with him. During the handful of encounters I had with him on subsequent visits, he remained bashful though not unfriendly, and would stand for a while and respond shyly to queries about how he was before wandering off again. Any efforts to engage him in discussion about services or re-housing left him looking helplessly at

Eilin, who would waft him away ignoring these intrusions, and lapse back into her memories.

Her father, Paidi, was a neat lean man, with a ruddy elongated face and a dark moustache which he always kept neatly trimmed. He would put a fresh coat of paint on his old sidecar every summer and bring out the faded tartan rug, which her mother would have washed and ready. He was an entirely different class of a man to his own father, Paidi Mor, who had been big and angular. Paidi was small and wiry, but strong and very good natured. Any fine day and he would be off to Kilrush to meet the steamer from Limerick where he'd pick up the holiday-makers from Cappa Pier and take them to Kilkee. He'd often take her up with him though her sister Bride would be mad, saying that she'd got to do all the jobs while Eilin got away with murder. 'Sure she's only little, and doesn't take up a payin seat in the car," Paidi would say soothingly, giving her a surreptitious wink.

She loved the excitement of it all, "We must get to the passengers before Sean Ban bates us to it Eilin," he'd say, his eyes sparkling, and on arriving at the little pier would throw the reins to her, leaping onto the steamer as she berthed. There he'd proclaim to the passengers that "he had a, fine commodious car and the fashtest horse in all of Clare." *The Lord and his Blessed Mother preserve us,* but she used to be terrified as they raced Sean Ban all the way to Kilkee. She would yell, "Don't, Daddy, don't," but he'd pay no attention, and she never forgot the day he winkled past Sean Ban's superior car just as they were coming into Kilkee. She thought it was the end of them and the oul car rattling away beneath them. But sure that's the way it was with them, they'd force another car off the road as they raced to Kilkee or were forced off in their turn. All that mattered to them was getting ahead of the other drivers no matter if all were killed! It was great to see the sea when they got there, and the seagulls dancing in the wind above the ocean.

It was during these drives that her father told her the stories that still haunted her memory. There was one very wet evening, when they stopped to listen to a skeletally thin dark youth, with the rain sheeting down his ragged jacket and trousers and his coal black hair glistening in the flickering gaslight. He threw back his head and sang …

But once more returning
Within our veins burning
The fires that illumined dark Aherlow's glen
We raise the old cry anew
Slogan of Con and Hugh
Out and make way for the bold Fenian men

She thrilled to the words, and Paidi told her solemnly that the songs let people say what they felt when they'd be frightened to say them straight out. He said that the Fenians were strong silent, not boastful men, who cared passionately for their country and were prepared to die for it. He had spent much of his young life with cousins near Mallow in Cork where patriotism and Fenian activity flourished. He used to watch them going up to drill in the woods of an evening and wished he could go along with them. He remembered racing down the main street one hot summer afternoon to the corner of the lane where the local baker lived and watching through the windows as the constables searched the house. They cheered when the constables announced that nothing had been found to compromise the prisoner, and sure that was no wonder, he said, because there were sworn Fenians among the constables. On the way back from Kilkee they'd collect seaweed to fertilise their little garden. In her grandfather's time, he used to have to look for some out of the way place when he was collecting anything from the shore. If he was seen, the landlord would make him pay for it. She recalled Paidi's words, "Greed is a terrible cruel thing girl," and remembered how he'd spit out his tobacco juice in anger at what he called their spite against the poor trying to improve their miserable lot.

I glanced through the cracked filthy window at a lowering sky and set off home. The images of Eilin's harsh story still fresh, I felt faintly ashamed to be thinking of supper, but I was hungry. There was some *porc a la crème* left over from my supper party the previous night. The recipe for this, culled from my one and only cookery book, had been a great success. It was my first attempt to entertain since I'd come to Kilrush some two months before, and I was pleased when Maggie and Michael O'Dea accepted my invitation. A warm-hearted kindly couple who ran the local fish and chip shop, they had made me very welcome since my arrival, and their home had become a refuge. It was a good night, and I relished the sly but generous humour with which, they regaled me with the foibles of the various town worthies. They were very much grounded in their community, and I found their lack of reverence a refreshing antidote to the slightly pious respect which my role was usually accorded. I was riveted when they spoke of the famine mentality which characterised so many of the old people whose parents would have suffered grievously during those years. "Sure, they'd rather starve, the creatures, than part with the bit of money they'd saved," Maggie explained, because however irrational it might seem now, for them, money still meant insurance against the workhouse and eviction.

I thought of Eilin…

CHAPTER 3

A Legacy of Famine

The lyrics of Bob Dylan's *Mr. Tambourine Man* blasted out as I made my way along the winding West Clare roads.

> *Take me on a trip upon your magic swirlin' ship*
> *My senses have been stripped, my hands can't feel to grip*
> *My toes too numb to step, wait only for my boot heels*
> *To be wanderin*

There was a bit of that magic around the previous night at the Crosses of Anna up near Quilty. I hadn't known what to expect as I made my way to the rather Spartan pub, located at a crossroads traditionally associated with dancing in Clare. Inside seemed to match the bleak exterior; a big plain room with narrow benches set back against the wall, and the barman serving drinks behind the bare counter. There was a good number of men and women sitting or standing around while an accordionist sat at his ease in one corner. They were solid farming folk, a bit old-fashioned in their dress and mostly middle-aged. As I entered, the music struck up, and they moved into sets of four couples. I stared in astonishment as this staid gathering transformed itself into a lively, almost skittish display of complex rhythmic step-dancing and graceful movement. I was delighted when a few of the men took me up for some of the dances and had begun to get the hang of them by the evening's end.

Eilin loved it when she and Paidi stopped at Maher's little establishment, part shop, part pub and part sitting room, on their way home from Kilkee. She would settle herself on the bench by the wall relishing her cup of milk in the flickering light of the turf fire, and listening to her father's stories and those of his friends and neighbours. One evening when Schooner Breen, the travelling fiddler, noticed her foot tapping out the rhythm of his lively jigs and reels, he insisted that she must dance to them. She was shy at first, but Mrs Maher, the solemn-faced widow who owned the establishment, came out from behind the counter and told her she'd teach her a few steps. She found it easy to get the hang of them, and they all said that soon she'd be the best dancer in all of Clare. She was surely surprised to see old Mrs Maher, who must have been near enough seventy then, keep step to a lively horn-pipe before they had to leave for home. Old Dan Breen told them that there had never been a finer dancer in all of Ireland than Mary Maher as a young girl, "and sure isn't she still as good as ever," he said, and he kissed her hand. She was surprised to see the old lady blush, something she'd never seen an old person do before.

Some years after my spell working in Kilrush, I would bring the Scottish friend who would become my husband to a very similar establishment in the village of Doonaha on the Loophead side of Kilkee. He was enchanted by the tiny bar cum shop and the old car seats snuggling up to the warm peat fire in the grate. There was a ladder leaning up outside the counter to a little attic room that seemed to have been built out over half the roof-space. A small boy climbed up there at one point, maybe to do his homework. Paidi and Eilin would have been very at-home.

The music was a great comfort to them, and thanks be to God and his Blessed Mother they were never short of it. Her father was a good singer and also had a share of the old Gaelic airs and songs that were beginning to die out then. Whenever there was a gathering of any kind, he'd be asked to go along and would bring her with him. Her mother Annie wasn't happy about what she called her father's gallivantin, and many's the night he returned from some gathering with the drink on him to a cold reception. There were a lot of American Wakes back then, to say goodbye to neighbours who left for America when they didn't know if they'd ever see them again. These were great fun, but when she began to realise that they were losing their friends and neighbours, maybe forever, the merriment was mixed with a lot of sadness. The famine led to a decline in wakes for people when they died, and the priests didn't agree with them either; said they were disrespectful, but sure they used to think it a mark of disrespect not to attend the house where the corpse was laid. Paidi told her of the grand nights altogether that they used to have in his father's time. After the rosary and a respectable amount of keening, there'd be some great songs and stories, and even a bit of dancing. There would be good whiskey too and platefuls of tobacco for the clay pipes that people smoked then, and many was the story told of the departed friend, which was surely a comfort.

Her parents weren't easy with one another, and she'd often catch the wary, slightly pleading look with which her father responded to the withdrawn aspect her mother nearly always wore. She knew that he hadn't expected the prematurely greying hair and morose appearance when he first welcomed his dark bride to his trim cottage. She had been delighted with everything then; the solid stone walls, the stands of elders and hawthorn bushes sheltering the cottage, and the stone flagged floor, so different to the poor mud cabin she'd grown up in. He remembered her swinging the cast iron crane over the open fire and marvelling at the number of pots and pans he had. "I never thought we'd have such a grand house Paidi," she had said, leaning her elbows on the deal table and sitting down on one of the four sugan chairs made especially for his wedding. They had two bedrooms as well as the kitchen and a separate shed for the horse and the pigs. He was proud and happy to see her delight and to know that it had been in his gift. The change was very sudden.

It was after the birth of their eldest son Dan that Annie became fearful. Time and again Paidi asked her what was wrong, but she just shook her head and cried as if her heart would break. Poor Paidi had been delighted at his son's birth and was bewildered by her despair. He asked his sister Maggie to come and talk to her. Maggie was a great woman for the fun, and he recalled that the day she came over, there was a hen hiding under one of the chairs waiting to lay an egg, and it being wet and windy he hadn't the heart to put her out. To tell the truth, he hadn't the heart for anything that time, he was that worried about his wife. Maggie was also a great one for the sayings and when she saw Annie so down she'd said, "Musha Annie you're only a short time in this life, and it's your folly if you don't borrow from it," but that didn't do a bit of good. Annie remained very listless, though she got a bit better as the years went on. Paidi thought that she could never get over the horrors she'd known.

Eilin was only eight or nine when Paidi brought her to see the pauper's grave in a corner of the old Work-house in Kilrush, where so many of her mother's people were buried. Though grassed over by then, it had been a big open trench where the bodies of the poor were put in layers, one over the other, including the Madden family who were related to Annie. They had to seek help there in 1849 because the outdoor relief stopped that year, and they had no money to pay the rent. They'd always managed up to then, even through the hard years of 1846 and '47, and the priest himself asked the landlord to wait, but no, the Lord have mercy on his black soul, there was nothing for it, but they had to get out of their cabin, which was pulled down around them. The worst of it was that her grandfather had offered the family shelter in his cabin, but the bailiffs threatened to evict him and all his family too if he did this. It was said that the landlord wanted them out because he'd have less rates to pay if he had fewer cabins on his land. Sure that time, there were hundreds and hundreds put out like that. Paidi told her how pitiable it was, to see them try to protect themselves from the elements in the scalpeen they built. They made it by digging a hole in the earth and covering it with some of the boards from their old cabin, but with the cold wet November bringing icy winds, it provided little shelter, and they had no recourse but the workhouse.

It was the death of their little six-month-old son that triggered their final despair. Mary Madden had gone out that morning to beg some milk from a local farmer who still had two cows. When she returned, she removed the tattered old blanket that covered the child's emaciated little body. It shivered just the once and was still. Mary knew he was dead, but she never cried, just wrapped the dead child in an old blanket and held it till Dan Madden came home. He looked long at his little son, but never shed a tear either, sure maybe they thought he was better off out of this sorry world. He dug a hole in the back-garden of what had once been their cabin to bury his child while her grandfather went to get the priest.

Eilin's mother was taken to see them in the workhouse and never forgot what she saw. There were lines of carts parked in front, with old people and children stretched out on the straw, waiting to get in. They were famished and ragged, and so far gone with the fever and dysentery that they could neither walk nor stand. The three little Madden boys shared one small bed in the infirmary, where they died not long after. Sharing, two or three to a bed was common then, because of the huge numbers of people desperately seeking shelter and food. It was bitterly cold in the workhouse, and it was no great wonder that the increased wave of deaths in the spring carried with it the whole Madden family. They'd known they'd not come out; it was called the slaughter house because folk not dead on arrival certainly died there. Their people didn't even know when they died, and there'd be no wake at that time. The wake used to be a powerful comfort to the people, where sadness and memories were shared and the life celebrated. In any case, neither friend nor family could have gone, had they known, as they were barely surviving themselves.

Wasn't it a terrible thing that ne'er a prayer was said by their gravesides, nor anyone to shed a tear, just thrown in, one on top of the other, like bits of oul rubbish?

Her father used to recite a verse culled from *The Nation* newspaper ...

> *Aye, buried like dogs are the poorhouse dead*
> *in this Christian land without shroud or shred*
> *of a winding sheet on the wasted frame*
> *and this Godless thrift is our Guardian's aim.*

The emaciated bodies, twisted mouths and tormented eyes of hunger were everywhere, as was the stench of death, and all around them, the countryside was littered with corpses. Their slow painful deaths were not recorded and meant nothing to the landlords. Paidi raged bitterly too against those well-off Catholic farmers and merchants who wanted to keep the rates down rather than provide the money needed to help their despairing fellow countrymen so that even the pitiful relief of the workhouse was denied to many. Forty of her mother's starving neighbours and relatives crossed Poulnasherry bay from Moyarta to Kilrush to seek relief one cold December day in 1849 only to be turned away because it was already overcrowded. Thirty-five of them drowned when their boat overturned on the return journey that wintry night, and maybe it was a blessing to have a quicker end to their misery. Well, they were surely bad days.

There was the odd story that would put heart into you. Just a couple of years before she was born the McGrath family put up a ferocious resistance when the local landlord, Captain Vandeleur, tried to evict them. That was in 1888 when there was more fight in the people, and young McGrath broke out of the handcuffs they put on him three times, so great was his rage. They had the backing of Michael Davitt and the land league by then, but best of all was the presence of a Dublin photographer Robert French. Didn't he take photographs of the evictions that were plastered all over the press. That made them sit up, and the matter was even raised in the House of Commons. This shamed the blackguard, and he called a halt to the evictions, indeed all twenty-two families that were evicted that month of July in 1888, were able to return to their holdings.

I was saddened to hear that Eilin's mother never got over her fear of eviction. In spite of her assertion that she and Sonny would not end up in an *oul scalpeen*, I would discover how enduring were the long shadows cast by these inherited memories, when, a few months later, Eilin was admitted to Kilrush hospital with pneumonia. The nurse on the ward told me of how distraught she had been when the men went to lift her onto the stretcher. In spite of her weakness, they had to hold her down. She was delirious and kept muttering that she didn't want to go into the workhouse, that she could pay. All their efforts to explain that it was the hospital she was being taken to could not budge her terror, or her conviction that she was being removed to the old workhouse. I felt an aching pity for that terror, recalling her account of Annie's unshakeable fear that they might end up in the workhouse.

Promising to come again soon after that visit, I smiled to recall Eilin's response. "Do to be sure child, isn't it grand talking to you, and maybe the next time I'll cook a goose for you, and sure you'd never know maybe you and Sonny will make a match of it."

CHAPTER 4

Childhood Wins Through

The ferocious briny wind reaching in from the Atlantic tangled my hair as I strode along Doughmore strand. I glanced up at the lone man calling to the red setter puppy racing toward me and smiled at the joyful swirl of legs and tail.

It was the respite I needed to clear away the images of misery left by a recent visit to a remote, unhappy little home where neither parent was prepared to send their ten-year-old son to school. The thin, tired woman and her barrel-chested husband had greeted me with an impenetrable wall of wariness. There was a cow bawling in the background, and he was clearly impatient to be attending to her and her missing calf. I had worked in a deprived housing estate in Dublin where I was as likely to get abuse as a welcome. Somehow I had found that easier to deal with, than the blank wall of passivity encountered in some of my West Clare clients. I found my dealings with the parents of children failing to attend school particularly frustrating. Efforts to get alongside them often met with little success, and their response seemed to be underpinned by a deep-seated distrust. I would be regaled with a list of ailments that had kept him/her from attending in the face of which, I felt very helpless. It was only when I spoke of the legal requirement that could lead to a compulsory order, that a level of uneasy acquiescence was achieved. I always felt soiled by having to resort to what were in effect, threats, and which must have linked me in their eyes to a long line of hated authority figures. I was becoming aware of the defences, cloaked by a superficial friendliness, which characterised a number of the situations I was dealing with and I struggled to grapple with some of the reasons for this.

I sensed a similar wariness in Eilin, and would discover that it was the fears that had haunted her mother which generated the miasma of anxiety that continued to shroud her life. Fear of any kind of illness was particularly terrifying, and no doubt traceable to her grandmother's death from typhus, when her mother Annie was just five years old.

> She knew that her grandmother had to be removed from the house. Her grandfather had cleared out the shed where their pig used to sleep and put in clean wooden planks and a straw mattress. An aunt had covered this with some old clothes and a couple of blankets which she'd got from the doctor's wife, and made her as comfortable as she could. She used to come and look after her and bring her gruel every day. Annie would stand outside the shed and call into her mother asking when she'd be better while the poor woman would reply that, with God's mercy it would not be long now. After a while, her mother didn't answer at all, and one of her older sisters came and pulled her away into the cabin, crying herself. Annie had known, without being told, that her mother was gone. She stayed in her bed all that day, and nobody bothered her. The priest came to the house and said some prayers, but there was no wake or funeral. She was buried in a simple wooden box made by her husband; there was no money to buy a coffin.

Eilin's mother never cried when she spoke of her grandmother's death, but she sobbed and sobbed when she spoke of the death of another young woman, Maggie, a stranger to the area who had died just a mile down the road from their cabin. Maggie used to work as a housemaid for old Mrs Kennedy, the publican's wife, and Annie recalled the wintry day in Kilrush when she saw her leaving the public house with her shawl pulled tightly around her and a small ragged bundle under her arm. She described the long dreary straggling street, with piles of muck everywhere, and most of the half doors in the dingy buildings lining the street shut tight against the sleety down-pour. Maggie was crying and very pale as she stepped, without any help, into Tadg Flynn's cart. Annie and her father went into the public house then and asked Mr Kennedy where Maggie was going. He looked very uneasy but told them that she wasn't well and that they couldn't have her in the house for fear of infecting the children. They'd arranged, he said, for her to live in a place apart until she was well again.

They would discover later, that she was taken to the bog near their house where a hut had been built for her, and the floor covered with straw. Into this, she was placed without a stick of furniture other than a bucket, and a small gallon of water. Dr. Ryan called to their cabin the following day after visiting poor Maggie, and her father told her that he d never seen him so distressed. He had, he said, seen many's the ugly thing but never thought to see the like of that; a poor sick young woman thrown on straw that barely covered the ground and it full of puddles, and not a soul to tend her. Dr. Ryan was a good man and offered money out of his own pocket to anyone who would help nurse her but could find no-one; sure they were fearful for their own families. Only the doctor and the parish priest vis-

ited, and she died after two days in that lonely hut.
Though she had been a stranger to her, it was the
memory of this young woman that unleashed the reser-
voir of sadness her mother had accumulated over a
harsh life.

Eilin stood up suddenly, peering out of the dirty little window at the dripping hedge. I could see the bony ridge of
her thin spine through the threadbare cardigan she
clutched around her. She turned and smiled unexpectedly:
"Musha child what business have I to be telling you all
these sad stories when you should be out enjoying yourself
and not listening to an old crone like me. The next time
you come, we'll talk about the Kilkee races and Mikey."

They would pile into the sidecar early in the morning
and set off for Kilkee, delighted when they got the first
salty whiff off the Atlantic. Sean let out a yelp of excitement when they glimpsed the town snuggled
around the great horseshoe bay, and pulled Dan with
him to race over the sands. Her father made his way
round to his cousin Paddy Considine's house, in one of
the little side lanes which ran down to the sea. There,
he left the sidecar and let old Bob have the run of the
field behind their house. It was surely wonderful to
watch the horses racing along the sands at the edge of
the sea, and she knew that even before the existence of
the town, the people of southwest Clare used to gather
on the sand hills to enjoy the races. The course was
marked out by long poles with bright coloured flags
fluttering in the wind, and the horses 'galloping along
the edge of the water, their flying legs almost hidden by
the misty gauze whipped up by ocean spray, were a truly beautiful sight. There were all sorts of tents for
selling sweets and telling fortunes, and of course, Sean
and Dan entered the competition to stop the pig whose
tail was shaved and lathered. "Come on Dan we'll bate

the lads from Cooraclare this year," Sean shouted. Dan was a quiet shy boy, but he always went along with Sean, who had the stronger personality. It was funny to see how they threw off their jackets and dived for the pig's tail, and sure it wasn't long before they both landed face down in the sand.

She was about ten when she started entering for the shawl dances, so called, because in the old days, whoever won used to be given a shawl. A big ring would be formed around a platform and sometimes they'd have pipers and fiddlers playing, and sometimes just fiddlers. Some of these were easier to dance to than others, probably because their rhythm would be livelier and would make you want to dance. She'd often get second or third place but never won. A girl from Kilkee called Biddy Casey nearly always took first prize. She was the same age, and she remembered being very jealous of her and wishing that she'd go off to America. She used to try and make her feet and toes twinkle like hers but it was no good, 'twas like as if she had no bones in them they were so squiggly and sure, she was as graceful as a swan too, bad cess to her!

The best bit of the day out was when she got to see Mikey, who was Paddy Considine's son. He was a tall gangly lad with a shock of fair hair which always stuck up in the air and out over his ears. He was awful untidy, and his trousers always seemed a foot too short for him. She loved his eyes; they were wide, blue, and innocent and he had a way with him that you couldn't but like. He was a great favourite with everyone, and she'd always had a soft spot for him. She recalled the excitement of the great lolloping piggy back rides he'd take her on along the sands, as a child. As she grew older, she noticed the way he took pleasure in everything, whether it was a fine day for the fishing or a nicely finished stack of turf. It was only later she knew that it was the way you could be with him without having to talk to him all the time that was just fine.

She and her father would often spend the best part of the day with Mikey's family when they dropped the visitors in Kilkee. They were poor people and had a small thatched cottage, but it was always well swept, with their fishing gear stacked neat and tidy at the back of the kitchen. Paddy was proud of his little garden, keeping it well manured with seaweed. In it, he grew oats for his donkey and potatoes, cabbage and a few turnips for themselves. He and Paidi would sometimes go out in the currach, and they'd have a bit of fish to take home for the tea. When she'd asked him why the people didn't eat fish when they were starving during the lean years, he told her that the fish had never been very plentiful around those shores, and the currachs couldn't go too far out to sea without great danger. His face darkened in anger, as he added that the parish priest had tried to get the government to invest in boats and equipment that would have let the folk fish out in the deep, but sure they hadn't cared enough about them.

She was about fifteen when she asked Mikey if she could go with him to raise the lobster pots and help gather seaweed from the rocks over on the island. "You can to be sure," said Mikey. There wasn't a breeze in the sky, and the sea was calm. They spent a couple of hours on the island cutting the seaweed with a knife and sickle before they flung themselves on the beach tired out. "Now, isn't this grand," Mikey said, as he bit into the potato scones and took a swig from the bottle of milk they shared.

She knew that he was always happy to be with her, and even when she was a little girl, he would make time to play. Now that she was a young woman, he was shyer as they lay on the sands that day. Later, while idly toeing a pebble by the water's edge, she caught him glancing sideways at her through his tousled fringe. It was good to be near and to catch the salty smell of him that wafted on the breeze. "I'll race you to the rock by the Priest's cove and give you a count of ten start," he challenged. They pelted along the strand with Mikey stretching ahead of her as they reached the cove, where they both collapsed laughing. Her mouth became dry quite suddenly, and she was breathing very fast when he stopped laughing and looked at her in such a serious way, not at all like his usual self. After a minute, he turned away: "We'd better go back Eilin, but I'm glad you came," he said, simply. He needed to raise some lobster pots by the rocks at the lip of the cove for her father to sell in Kilrush, and she thought, "well bad cess to my father and his lobster pots."

The wind got up quickly on the way back; the sky and sea darkened, and white foam whipped up around the currrach. She shivered in the icy spray and could see that it took all Mikey's strength to keep the currach end-on to the huge waves. She looked fearfully at the thick bed of seaweed covering the bottom of the currach with those strange looking lobster creatures and wondered how anyone would want to eat them. As the wind gathered force around them. Eilin could see that Mikey was tiring. The menace of the heaving ocean recalled the many stories of friends and relatives lost at sea, and they were both very silent. "Jesus, Mary and Joseph help us, Jesus, Mary and Joseph help us," she whispered over and over, fearful that they were going to drown. The relief of seeing the sands of Kilkee approaching gave Mikey more heart. He took a firmer grip of the oars and with a great spurt of energy, put his back into the pulling. Paidi and Paddy were at the shore on the lookout for them and helped to pull the currach up. "Run like the divil up to the house the pair of ye," Paddy shouted, "and change them clothes and get some warmth into ye." It was the great welcome Mrs Considine had for them as she fed them strong sweet tea and brown bread with lashings of butter.

I was lulled into a slightly hypnotic trance by the warmth of the car and the thud, thud of the rackety old wipers swishing over and back, as I drove through the relentless rain. I barely caught a glance of the flying shape that whizzed by the front windscreen, before I braked wildly at the mighty thump on the right-hand side of the bonnet. The little car juddered to a halt, and I could see the fine plump pheasant futilely flapping one wing, in the ditch where it had fallen. I stared in dismay; I knew I should kill it and put it out of its misery, but I couldn't. Then, up an incline across the road, I noticed some men working on the roof of a house; they seemed to be building everywhere in Ireland at that time. I called over to them and explained what had happened pointing to the pheasant "Would you be able to kill it for me?" I asked a touch shame-facedly, "and maybe take it home to eat." "Indeed and I will," one of them said, "That will give the wife a nice surprise." I wasn't so sure, not many folk plucked and cleaned fowl now. So much for feminism, I thought wryly, but nonetheless relieved, and set off again.

CHAPTER 5

Growing Up and American Wakes

Listening to the Beatles song *Lucy in the Sky with Diamonds* as I drove towards Doonbeg, I wondered what on earth Eilin would make of the surreal lyrics …

> *Picture yourself on a train in a station*
> *With plasticine porters with looking glass ties*
> *Suddenly someone is there at the turnstile*
> *The girl with the kaleidoscope eyes …*

"Dan, Dan, there's a great job to be had with the railway." Eilin could still hear the excitement in her mother's voice. She had heard that there were jobs going on the new line which had opened up between Ennis and Kilkee, and she'd got an application form in the post office. Annie thought they should apply for Dan; it would be a grand government job with a pension and all. After they'd sent it off, didn't she get worried that maybe he'd be too quiet, and wouldn't pass the interview, so they told Sean to go instead, but to remember to call himself Dan because the application was in Dan's name. Well, off Sean went, and got the interview all right, but had to call himself Dan from then on. People didn't seem to notice or care about that sort of thing in the old days, you probably couldn't do it now, she sighed, things were more complex now. Afterwards didn't Sean get a great job looking after the level crossing for the railway, and a grand house for himself and his family into the bargain.

The interview was a great event, and Sean acquired a new suit for the occasion. There was a travelling tailor working in Kilrush at the time, who agreed to come out to the house to make it up for him. Jack McNamara was his name, and he used to say that he'd *build* him a suit, as if 'twas a house he was making. He was a stocky dark man with a very twinkly face, and he'd sit up on top of the table cross-legged, something that she only ever saw him doing, with his thimble, scissors, measure and materials all around him. The neighbours would gather of an evening when he was there as he had a great fund of stories. *Them who travelled were storied,* was a great saying of his, but that 'twas a hard life being driven from place to place. Indeed and he didn't look as if it was a hard life, as he was a right merry man and used to have everyone laughing at his stories, and didn't he build Sean a grand suit.

It was 1906, and she must have been about sixteen when she went over with her father to the wake at Maher's. It was to be an American wake for Peadar Maher who was leaving for New York the following morning. Her sister Bride was gone to England by then to work, and Sean was working on the railway, so it was just Dan and herself who went with Paidi. The Mahers were small farmers, but her father always said that Dick Maher was the best farmer in Clare. She liked their long low cottage, which always seemed cleaner than other folks' houses. The walls were whitewashed with a bit of that blue dye that gave them a shining quality, and their haggard was tidy with a long hay rick and the stacks of turf neatly tied down for the winter. There were barrels of porter lined up behind the back door when they arrived and a deal of young men holding up the gable end

39

of the house, smoking and chatting together. Inside was cosy too, and colourful, which was something unusual back then. Mrs Maher was a wiry busy little woman whose black hair, already streaked with grey, always seemed to be escaping from the bun she tried to keep it in. She was a great knitter, and there were red and green shawls thrown over the chairs and benches. She used to play the fiddle, and Eilin knew that she had been taught by the blind travelling fiddler Schooner Breen. That night she was sad, and sure it was no wonder, with her youngest son heading so far away the next day, and not knowing when, if ever, she'd see him again.

The white scrubbed table was pulled back under the window, and the flagged floor cleared for a set by the time they arrived. Paidi, who was a great one for the Clare set, swept her into the dance straight away, and she hardly stopped all night. There was a lot of whiskey and porter drunk by the men, and young Paddy Sullivan got very bold. His father owned a pub inside in Kilrush, and Paddy was like him, a low-sized stocky lad with freckles and red hair, but a great dancer, and it was he who whirled her around for most of the evening. Mind you, he had wandering hands, and they wandered more as the night went on, so that she was forever telling him to keep them to himself. Sure God didn't give me hands to do nothin with, he'd said, which made her laugh and she thought him great gas. Tim Kelly and some other fiddlers were there and with them a young girl about her own age, knocking a great tune out of an old squeeze box. Years later, this girl would marry Miko Crotty, who came back from America with money enough to buy a public house in the square in Kilrush. Mrs Crotty was to become a famous concertina player, and she would relish the great music they used to hear on the occasional nights they'd gather there.

"Where was Mikey that night," I asked her. "Oh he was there, to be sure he was, but he was very shy, and you couldn't get him to dance." "Well, he can't have been too happy seeing you having a great old time with the bould Paddy." "Yerra I didn't care, I was having great fun," was the heartless response. In any case, she saw him when they were leaving, still at the gable end of the house, and hardly able to stand up with the amount of porter he had in him.

I glanced at the sky heavy with dark pewter clouds and said I must be off. I stepped over the potholes along the lane which were full of liquid dung and reached the car before the rain began falling furiously aslant the windscreen. Driving back, hungry myself, I wondered if Eilin and Sonny lived exclusively on white bread and sliced ham, which was all I ever saw in the house. Their only way of cooking would be the old iron kettle, or a big pot over the fire, which they maybe cooked potatoes in. Eilin often threatened to cook a goose for me, and while I always thought she was joking, I was to learn afterwards that she did in fact, occasionally cook a goose in her pot oven. This was a huge squarish pot which would be placed over the fire on a kind of trivet, and hot sods of turf would be piled around it, and laid on top of the lid. A neighbour was to tell me that it tasted delicious, and that enjoyment of it was only marred by the fact that her thirteen cats would all gather round just when it was ready for eating.

I tried to get her to accept delivery of a hot meal a few days a week, but Eilin wouldn't hear of it. She seemed fearful of strangers coming to the house and had a positive allergy to anything that had the slightest whiff of the dreaded "charity".

41

CHAPTER 6

Dan Decides to Go

I looked at my watch; it was barely six o'clock, and I'd been listening to the distinct clip clop of horses and ponies this past half hour. Dragging my unwilling body from the bed, I went to look out over the square. I delighted in the timeless scene that met my gaze. It was the morning of the Kilrush horse fair, and there were hundreds of horses, ponies and donkeys pulsating within the confined space of the square. Men everywhere were arguing, and laughing, cursing and spitting as they prodded the animals the better to inspect them. Very soon the stall-holders arrived to set up shop all along Frances Street, selling an array of household utensils, clothes and all sorts of farm produce such as potatoes, vegetables, eggs, homemade jams, butter and cakes. I picked my way along the road fouled by animal dung, straw and mud. Why, on God's earth, had I worn my smart new flared trousers, now all mucky and limp? Later that evening, I would be glad I had taken the trouble to make my way to the cake stall, where I purchased a promising looking fruit cake.

Eilin's mother thought that it was because Bride was putting ideas into Dan's head that he wanted to leave. Bride had been working as a maid over in London for a few years now. She had learnt to talk different and had fine new clothes and shoes, and they thought that she was becoming very fancy. There was a fair in Kilrush

42

one time she was home, and she, Dan and herself had taken eggs in to sell. You could hardly move for the animals all huddled together in rough pens. "The stink is terrible," Bride said, holding her nose, but they just laughed at her. They were used to it. They watched the men pushing and poking the cattle and sheep and arguing about their price as they listened to the pigs squealing fit to burst, with their hind legs tied together. The big square was covered in dung, and Bride noticed it squishing up through Dan's boots with the toes and sides out of them. You need to get new boots, Dan, she said, but he replied that they'd have to do him a while, "as the oul' man hasn't had much luck with the sidecar business since they brought in the railway." Well didn't Bride go and buy him boots, and she could that see that this embarrassed him though he'd been glad enough of them.

As they walked home, Bride talked of how she liked it over in England, the way you could meet loads of people, some of them from very far away places and most of them friendly. She told them that it was great to have a bit of money to get what you needed, and Eilin, who'd never had any money, thought longingly of such independence. Bride described the Irish dances where you could go at the weekend and the pubs where the Irish would go for a drink so that it wasn't too lonely at all. Dan asked her if she missed home, and she said, sure I do sometimes and it's grand to come home, but after a while it's all the same, and everyone is so poor that I'm glad to go back.

This clearly got Dan thinking, but it was Mary Moloney who finally decided him to go. Eilin heard them talking after Mass at St Martin's well, where a great crowd of them had gone down for the pattern, to do a few rounds of the Holy Well and have a bit of fun. Long ago the old folks used to kill a pig or a goose and rub the blood on their houses to protect themselves and their livestock, but a lot of the old customs died out after the famine, and sure the priests didn't like them anyway. Mary had gone along with herself, Dan, and Sean who had the day off from the railway. Her mother grumbled about why they wouldn't go to St Senan's well in Kilkee, which was just down the road, instead of wearing out the poor oul horse with their gallivantin. Poor Annie, sure they paid no heed and set off in great spirits. It wasn't a lonely road to be sure, between meeting cart loads of neighbours and relations, and Sean telling funny stories about the people he met on the railway. He sang them a new song by someone with a strange name, *Percy French,* and she could still recall a verse or two of it …

> *You may talk of Columbus's 'sailin'*
> *Across the Atlantical sea*
> *But he never tried to go 'railin'*
> *From Ennis as far as Kilkee*
> *You run for the train in the 'mornin'*
> *The excursion train 'startin' at eight*
> *You're there when the clock gives the 'warnin'*
> *And there for an hour you'll wait …*

They stayed with the Considines in Kilkee that night and had a grand bit of music and a good few sets with Paddy Lynch playing the fiddle. She remembered it well because it was the first time Mikey had danced with her. He held her nice and tight around the waist the way you wouldn't fall or trip, and he held on to her afterwards as if he didn't want to let her go; oh she'd been happy that night. It was Sean as usual who had started them off. "Give us an oul tune Paddy," he said, grabbing Mary, "and let you and me bate the smithereens out of them oul flagstones Mary." Dan just sat watching the dancing, but Eilín knew that Mary was looking at him, and she'd always known that it was to Dan she was drawn, though it was Sean who seemed to take up with her at dances.

The following morning they were up early and on the road which was crowded with lots of other pilgrims. Halfway there, they pulled in at Sean McNamara's licensed premises, where the men ordered a gallon of porter to be distributed amongst them; sure no-one would serve you a gallon of porter now, would they? She and Mary contented themselves with a bottle of lemonade. It was time for Mass when they reached St Martin's well, and afterwards, they did a few rounds of the well and said the rosary. When that was over there was great talk and laughter, and Mikey took her down to where a rocky ledge overlooked the ocean. He held her hand and told her she was growing up to be a fine girl, and wouldn't it be the lucky man who'd get her. It was then that she heard Dan's voice: "Would you to be sure Mary?" and her saying, "Sure and indeed and I will Dan, but I'll wait till the hay is in, and by then you'll own the place and be able to look after me," and Dan laughed. They were on a ledge underneath them, and she made Mikey promise to leave them alone, because he was all for going down to tease them, and she knew Dan wouldn't like that.

Dan was different after and talked openly about going to London. He wasn't really sad anymore, though he didn't say a word about Mary. There were a lot of folk emigrating back then and it was exciting but sad too, especially for the old people. Dan was about twenty-four when he made his way to Dublin, before catching the night packet for Holyhead. Bride had written from London to tell him that there were jobs to be had, building the London underground, and sent him money for the fare. He went back to school for a few months before going, to try and improve his English as a lot of the young men who were emigrating did, to equip them better for their new lives. Most of them still spoke Irish at home even though they'd all learnt English at school. Dan's reading and writing in English had never been much good, the words all seemed to get mixed up on him.

He was her mother's favourite; his quiet ways seemed to soothe her. "Sure why do you have to be going Dan, aren't you all right the way you are," she said, when he first mentioned going. "In the name of God what's there here for him Annie?" Paidi asked. "We can hardly live off the few spuds and cabbage we grow ourselves, and now that the new railway is bringing the visitors from Ennis to Kilkee there's no longer much call for the sidecar business," Annie replied that the odd bit of money they got from the others that were away was enough to keep them going, and Paidi said no more. He knew that Dan had made up his mind to go, and he was glad of it as there wasn't much work to be had in West Clare and he'd worried that Dan might not have the stomach to leave. By this time Bride had been back home for a couple of visits and was full of the excitements of her new life. She talked about the railways and trams and her lovely new clothes. Clare was such a backward place, she said; she was surprised that there was anyone left in it. Eilin knew that she was beginning to get restless herself.

The day before Dan left, she went out with him to cut and bring home some turf. There was a whole line of turf cutters stretched out along the bog that day, their sleans momentarily glinting as the light caught them in mid-swing. It was a grand day, full of golden glimmerings where the sun shone on the little pools of water.

The men were cutting the sods and the girls and younger boys were stacking them up to dry. It was a clear frosty night, and the moon was already up by the time they walked home by the little river. It was all swollen then by rain, and so silent. They followed the line of tired men carrying their shovels over their shoulders like rifles, and Dan was very quiet. She knew he was sad to be going away. That night as their mother trimmed the wick of the oil lamp before they knelt down to say the rosary, Eilin noticed Dan looking around the bare little house as if he wanted to remember it all. I'll not be long after you Dan, she said as they went to bed, little knowing then, that something was to happen which would set her feet in a very different direction, and take her a lot further from home.

She rose early on the morning he left, in order to accompany him to Kilrush where he was to get the train for Ennis, then Dublin. He would cross over by steamer from there to Holyhead. It was a beautiful morning, with a thin film of ice putting a gloss on the turf stack by the side of the cabin, and even the dung heap sparkled, caught in a shaft of pale sunlight. Annie was crying while Paidi harnessed old Bob to the sidecar. "Will you leave off Annie," he said, "Sure won't he be home before we know it, with the money jingling in his pocket." Dan was very quiet and didn't look at his mother as he got quickly up onto the sidecar. The curtain of mist that had shrouded the early morning cleared away quickly, and their spirits lifted as they rattled along to Kilrush.

I was feeling pretty dismal myself as I drove home that grey drizzly afternoon. Arriving at the door of my flat, I stared in amazement at the huge flagon of Chianti wine encased in its red, white and green raffia coat. It was a shaft of Mediterranean sunlight, and it sent my spirits soaring. I looked around for the friends who had carried it in their back-packs all the way from Tuscany.

It was some weeks previously that I had arrived alone in Venice for a holiday. My delight in the beauty of the fragile townscape, and the delicacy of the architecture reflected in its many canals was marred by continual harassment by an assortment of seedy characters. Meeting Jenny and Karen was a godsend. Jenny was an open-hearted, sturdy girl from Maine in New England who promoted the benefits of Transcendental Meditation with a missionary zeal. Karen, of New York Jewish background, was beautiful, dark and serene, and I revelled in their warm, light-hearted company. Now here they were. I felt very emotional, having never expected them to take me up on the invitation to visit such a remote location. It was way out-with their planned itinerary; and to think that they had lugged that heavy flagon of wine all the way. The few days we spent together drinking the Chianti and reminiscing about our shared time in Venice and Florence, washed the West Clare landscape with the colour and light of those magical places.

Chapter 7

America Beckons

On Sunday Maggie O'Dea and I went for a walk within the woodland of the crumbling Vandeleur estate. The breeze rustled quietly amid the chestnut leaves and a sense of reverence permeated the woods. It was a day of sun and showers, and our path was spangled with islets of light filtered through the delicate spring foliage. We allowed a seductive little path off to the side to insinuate us down to St Senan's well by the river. There we sat, hypnotised by the tortoiseshell water which rippled away merrily and watched as a herd of cows made their stately way down to a shallow part of the river. Maggie loved the estate for the trees and would always name them as she passed, sometimes putting her arms around a big trunk to hug it with human warmth. "They may have been ugly evicting landlords," she said, mindful of the sufferings of hundreds of families, "but we have to thank them for these."

Eilin had always loved the final harvesting of the hay. The summer before Mary went to join Dan in London was a wet one, and the hay had taken longer than usual to dry. By late August, the sun was hot in the sky, and the stubbled fields glimmered in a golden haze. All the neighbours gathered to help, creating neat little cocks weighted down with solid stones attached to the sugans. These would protect the hay in the face of the wet and windy weather to come. It would have been grand to be in the fields that day, but she had to help Mrs Moloney bake the spotted dicks and apple cakes for the workers. Mind you, they had a good feed themselves when they took the tin cans of hot, strong tea out to the men. She could still taste the currant bread and the grand fresh butter. The children ran up and down the haycocks and had a great old time and Mary and herself sat on top of a hay rick, taking a ride back to Moloney's haggard. It was then that Mary told her that she had heard that Mikey Considine was marrying Brigid O'Dea, and she got such a shock that she hit her; poor Mary; Mikey's treachery wasn't her fault.

Brigid O'Dea had come home from America a few years before and was working inside in her brother's public house in Kilrush. She was what her Daddy used to call a fine cut of a woman, with a big bosom, slim legs and a face that was handsome in a fleshy sort of a way, but sure, they thought she was old. She would have been in her mid-thirties, and they said that she brought bags of money home with her from America. Paidi told Annie that Brigid and Mikey were going to open a licensed premises in Kilkee, and she said, "Musha Paidi, isn't it a pity for Mikey that she's so much older?" "What harm, isn't she still a fine armful of a woman, and that money will help to keep him warm," he replied. Men were ugly greedy pigs, who cared for nothing except money, she thought angrily. She walked away up the fields and cried for a long time, but that got it out of her, and she didn't cry after. Her mother was kind to her that night "Don't be blaming him Eilín," she said "Hasn't he to hang on to life too. They say that his father can no longer work with the coughing and weakness that's on him. He'll need to go away to hospital soon, and Mikey will have to support his mother and young sisters with very little to be got from the fishing now."

That was the night she decided she'd go to America too, and make lots of money and come home and find a fine young fellow for herself.

It was April 1907 when she finally sailed for New York. Her father hadn't wanted her to go. He'd always had a soft spot for her, but at that time, she didn't think much of any man and was very determined. It was easy enough to arrange because her mother had a deal of cousins in New York, and one of them, Maisie McElligot, offered to help with the passage money. Her mother wrote to her and by the following spring, her ticket was booked. It was only years later, when she herself was struggling to earn her way in New York, that she came to appreciate what hardship and sacrifice this had cost Maisie and her husband, Jack. They worked long hard hours to support themselves and their family and could little afford the price of her ticket. She knew that the folks at home would never realise the sacrifices that loyalty to their families cost many generous exiles. Well, it was surely a right leap into the unknown.

Paidi was very quiet the day he drove her to Kilrush, to begin her journey by train to Queenstown harbour in Cork, and she knew that he was sad. She watched the spears of fresh green shooting up through the jaded grass in the fields, and the delicate leaves of the hawthorn bringing new life to the withered hedges. There were splashes of yellow marsh marigolds brightening the boggy fields. Her mother began to cry when she put her new brown case into the cart and hugged her as she patted her back. It was the only time she ever remembered her mother hugging her. She was just nineteen and now that the time had come, she felt a sense of panic; she was an ignorant country girl, and sure what did she know about New York, wasn't it another world entirely. What if she wasn't able to get a job, or if she couldn't do it properly or the people didn't like her; she'd never get to come home.

She didn't recall much about the journey. When she got out at a beautiful big station near the harbour, there were thousands of people milling around. Two men were striding up and down with boards tied to them, front and back, inscribed with the fares to Boston and New York. Hawkers were all around selling everything from food to cooking utensils and rosary beads. The porters rushed over and back to the ship carrying stuff, and the ship's engines and the hooting horns made a woeful noise altogether. She wanted to go home then and was crying when an old man took her by the arm. "I'll show you where to go *a'stor*, don't you be frettin now," he said, and that helped a bit. Looking back from the deck of the tender taking her out to the ship, she could see the train still standing there, and had to fight the urge to run back to it. There were crowds on the quays waving as she watched the backs of the drivers, their carts now empty, returning to Cork. She felt numb as they moved away from the sea wall and wasn't reassured when they came up against the awesome bulk of the ship that would take her to New York. She'd never seen anything so huge in her life and was sure she'd get lost in it.

Shuffling along among the throng she heard a cheery voice behind her "Make way there," and looking behind, she saw a big brawny young man carrying a canvas bag above his head, weaving his way through the crowd. He was handsome, with high cheekbones, curly brown hair and blue eyes and she learnt later that he was called Mairtin. He and his sister Peig came from back Dingle way and were returning to New York after a holiday home. The people seemed to give way to him until a small wizened man, in his fifties maybe, turned around to face him, dropping his own case. He was spluttering with indignation: "Didn't I pay me ticket too you big bostoon and why should I be letting you go ahead of me?" The big fellow dropped his bag and looked astonished. "By the holy smoke you're right," he said and beamed at the enraged little man, "and sure I'll see to it that you get on board before me." With that, didn't he lift him over his shoulder, and calling to the handsome woman who trailed behind him, "bring my bag Peg and this man's case," he carried him on board.

The little man was fit to explode, and the rest were bursting their sides laughing. After that, she felt better and went right down to the bottom of the ship where their bunks were. Peig, who was a sister of the big fellow called Mairtin, was given a bunk on the top row, and she wasn't happy, maybe because she was a bit heavy for the climbing. Eilin told her that she could have her bunk if she liked, as it was lower down. She had been a bit frightened of Peig at first for she seemed very sharp and sure of herself and didn't seem to notice her before she offered her the lower bunk, but was nice to her afterwards.

The voyage over was great, not like during the famine when people were packed into the bottom of the ships as if they were animals, with no bunks or proper food or ways of keeping clean. They had running water from taps and lavatories which she'd never seen before, and she thought them a great luxury. The food was good too, with porridge, soup and lots of bread and butter as well as meat most days, which she wasn't used to. It was fine weather nearly all the time except for one day and night when there was a storm. Their soup sloshed around on the long tables they ate at, but there was a ledge all round the table which kept most of it from getting on the floor. A lot of people were sick that day, and the smell in the dormitory was awful. Peig brought her up on deck, telling her that the only way not to be sick was to stay up there.

That huge ship was tossed about like a box of matches. She was frightened, listening to the saloon doors slamming shut and the ship creaking in the bawling wind. You could hear the children crying and the groans of men and women being sick. She thought fearfully of dying without anything to mark her grave and of the terrifying creatures waiting in the depths of that waste of water to make short shrift of her remains. She held on to a pillar as they gazed at the broiling ocean, and from the shadows of the deck behind them heard the thin wavery voice of an old man singing …

> *Through many dangers, toils and snares*
> *I have already come*
> *'Tis grace hath brought me safe thus far,*
> *And grace will lead me home…*

He wasn't Irish, but she felt exhilarated by the words.

She began to feel a fierce joy in the terrifying power of the storm. The great thing was that she hadn't been sick, and by then she and Peig were friends. Peig made her laugh and didn't seem to care about anything. She worked in a bar owned by an Irishman called Mick O'Meara in New York and told Eilin that her local parish priest didn't like this and wanted her to go and work for a good Catholic family whom he knew. "Sure I didn't want to go and work for any snotty nosed woman and her snotty kids," Peig told her, and she was a bit shocked because, in those days, you wouldn't want to go against the priests. "What did you say to him," she asked. "I just told him that Mr. O'Meara wanted to marry me and that I was thinking about it." "So are you going to marry him," "Yerra, I don't know I might, and then again I might not, sure maybe I could do worse for myself," and that was all she could get out of her. "Well isn't it many's the time a person's mouth broke his nose," Peig had added in the Irish!

On fine days, Mairtin sat on an old box on the deck. There he'd play the accordion with the little furious man he had carried on board playing the whistle alongside him. His name was Sean Grace, a slim dark man with heavy lidded eyes and a round ball of a head. By then he and Mairtin were the best of friends. Sometimes people would get up a set to dance, and when they learnt that she was a dab hand at the Clare set, they'd have her up teaching the others how to do it. All the girls took a great shine to Mairtin, and why wouldn't they, sure he was as merry as he was handsome, but Peig warned her that he was not to be trusted. She said that he had girls all over the place and that he never gave them another thought once they were out of sight. Well, she thought of Mikey then, and hardened her heart against Mairtin; she wasn't going to let any other man make a fool of her. Between the music and the dancing, watching the men playing cards and the chatting, the voyage flew by and in no time at all they were told to get their things all packed up because they'd be in New York the following morning.

They were on deck early on the morning of that late April day in 1907 when they sailed into New York harbour, and she watched excitedly as the fog began to lift and the city's startling skyline emerged with the light. She had seen picture postcards of it, but they hadn't prepared her for the reality of those towering buildings thrusting upwards. How could they remain so tall and still in the wind. They gazed in awe at skyscrapers soaring hundreds of feet into the sky, and at what she learnt later were the tall gothic towers of the celebrated Brooklyn Bridge. The sound of the ship's hooters from the other vessels crowding the wharves punctured the early morning din. She caught sight of the Statue of Liberty which she knew was a sign of hope for all the people trying to find a better life, and she hoped it would be that for her. The huge masts of the sailing ships and the funnels of the steamships dwarfed the smaller boats and barges. Peig pushed her up to the front of the crowd gathering on deck, explaining that they'd get through quicker if they were near the front. They'd let the first and second class passengers off first as they'd already been inspected on board, but all of them in steerage had to go through Ellis Island's registration process.

The shifting crush of bodies as they disembarked was even worse as they were funnelled into the ferries that would take them to Ellis Island to be vetted and registered. She was glad of Peig's closeness and carefree spirit then; what if they decided that she wasn't fit, or she said something that they didn't like. She'd heard of a man up in Ennis who had been sent back because he had a bad limp and everyone said he was a fine worker. Peig told her that most likely they'd think she was daft and admit her to the lunatic asylum. She was glad afterwards that she didn't know then that they would indeed chalk an X on your jacket if they thought you had mental trouble and could very well deport you. She hung on to her case as they were ushered upstairs. 'Just a minute." A uniformed guard, whom she later heard was a doctor, stopped her and quickly lifted her eyelid with a button hook. She felt physically sick; what was wrong? He waved her on and Peig, whom he also stopped, explained that he was testing for trachoma, an eye condition that leads to blindness and would mean certain deportation if found. She was shaken by this and bewildered by the number of men in white coats or military uniform, all staring intently at her and the other immigrants as they went up the stairs. Some folk were called over and had letters chalked on their clothes, which meant that they had spotted a problem such as breathlessness which could mean you had respiratory difficulties, for which a big R would be chalked on. If they noticed limping, they would scrawl an L, thinking you might be lame, and these people would be sent for further investigation. They didn't want immigrants who couldn't work.

They found themselves in a grand domed hall with huge semi-circular windows where they were directed to wooden benches with hundreds of others. Suddenly her name was called, and she was told to approach one of the three high desks manned by stern looking officials. A whole series of questions were fired at her in quick succession, and she was so nervous that she could neither remember the questions or answers, but they must have been all right because she was waved on down the stairs to the left of the desk. There was a pale middle-aged woman with an R chalked on her coat, crying as she descended the middle stairs, reserved for those whose possible problems had been noted. She felt a surge of pity for the poor woman, what if she was sent back and separated from her family. Would she never see them again; would they all return to whatever desperate circumstances they had wanted so badly to leave? Peig would tell her later that Martin's flute playing friend had an R chalked on his jacket and was directed down the same centre stair, but Martin had stayed close by him, and at the top of the stairs when the officials were occupied he quickly whipped off his jacket and turned it inside out, following Martin down with no mark visible.

Then there was no more time for sad thoughts; she was down the stairs, and there in the meeting hall was Maisie and her daughter Nancy waving to her: "Welcome to New York Eilin." It was strange that she never asked them how they recognised her. They had come over from Manhattan by ferry that morning to be there to greet her. The worry that this tiny wizened little woman with the worn hands and a slight limp might not like her melted away in the warmth of her welcome. She found herself laughing and crying, and Maisie had to lean up to pat her shoulder which made her laugh more. It was the relief she supposed. She said goodbye to Peig, who gave her the address of the public house where she worked.

She was silent on the journey back to Manhattan, lost in wonder at the strangeness of this new environment. The clamour from vendors of all kinds of wares, some in strange languages, alongside the trundling sounds of cabs and carts, the wheezing and snorting of horses and the plaintive cries of street urchins begging, was deafening. She was amazed to see so many black people; she had heard about black people of course, but when she saw them that first day, and they pure black, she didn't think they were real. She asked Maisie if they maybe polished themselves, and Maisie laughed and laughed till the tears ran down her face. She had surely been very ignorant then. The height of the tenement blocks and the fact that so many families lived together in the same building seemed somehow frightening. There were millions of people teeming all around as they rattled along in a cab to the Lower West side of New York. She had never seen anything the likes of it and wondered would she ever get used to it.

Here they stopped in front of the six storey tenement building on 11th Street where Maisie and Jack lived. They had to climb up about four sets of stairs to get there, and she was astonished to find that it was as small as the home she'd left behind in Clare. There were just two rooms opening off a kitchen, and she was to share one bedroom with Maisie's daughter Nancy. However, they had running water and an indoor toilet and, as Maisie told her, this was a great luxury, as their previous apartment in the Lower East side only had outdoor privies in the yard. There, it was the janitor's job to clean these out, but he had been none too conscientious, and they used to stink. Indeed, Eilin thought it a great luxury too, as these were conveniences she'd never had at home. She watched the long flame licking up the lovely wine coloured glass shade of the oil lamp, which Maisie was lighting (it had been given to her by an old employer and was her pride and joy), as they told her of the desperate conditions some of the earlier immigrants had to put up with in Five Points; a place they said was full of gangsters, open sewers, stray dogs and poor women whose faces bore the marks of their cruel lives.

She learnt later that the two sons, Johnny and Joe, had shared the bedroom until they left home on marrying while Nancy slept on a pull-out chair by the fire escape. They now had their own apartments nearby, and she thought that it must be hard for Nancy to have to share her nice room again. Most people back then had to share with a lot more than just one other, Nancy told her, and she didn't complain. Jack and Maisie were kind to her and introduced her to lots of other Irish people living nearby. Indeed, she came to know more Clare people in New York than she ever did in Clare. This was because a big proportion of the increasing numbers of Irish who settled near the expanding West Side docks, from the late 1860s, were from Clare. Jack was very proud of his home county and was a member of the Claremen's Association, which used to meet nearby in Flannery's Hall or Greenwich hall. At Christmas, he always bought a box of Dalcassian cigars manufactured by Clareman William Crowley.

Jack was a quiet humorous man whose tired eyes seemed to mock his smile. He always wore a long black coat and a black hat pulled low over his forehead. He loved his pigeons and Eilin liked to spend time with him on the tenement roof where he kept his coop. Pigeon keeping on the Lower West Side was very popular with the Irish, and many men had pigeon coops on the roofs of the tenements they lived or worked in. A lot of the men used to gamble on them back then but Jack never did, he just loved to fly them and stroke the soft grey and plum coloured feathers. Some men lost a lot of money gambling on the pigeons, which caused trouble as few families had spare money to waste.

Indeed, she didn't have too much time to enjoy her surroundings as it was very clear that Maisie and Jack expected her to find work quickly and to help with the rent. She became aware of how hard they all had to work to survive in this new world. It was with a good deal of trepidation that she set about trying to find employment.

CHAPTER 8

Domestic Service and Life in New York

I had been slightly alarmed by the amount of freedom I was given to carve out my role as a professional social worker in West Clare. As a fledgling professional the previous year in London, my practice had been circumscribed by close supervision and scrutiny. It seemed a seismic leap from that to my current level of responsibility and independence and I found it both exhilarating and a little terrifying. I was very appreciative of the massive amount of support extended by the church. The meeting I'd attended the previous evening had been announced throughout the diocese at Sunday Mass, and I was aware of the incalculable value of having the support of such an efficient network of communication at my professional beck and call. Commenting on this to my friend Maggie, the latter replied rather sardonically that it didn't hurt that I was a relative of the Bishop, but I felt that this was a bit cynical. Everyone seemed to know that I had been to the "Bishop's Palace" for supper some weeks ago. As a first cousin of my father's, he no doubt felt a sense of familial duty to extend the invitation. I had been resolutely determined not to kiss his ring, a custom surely not in the spirit of Christ's injunction to be the servant of all, and he had given no indication of surprise when I shook him energetically by the hand on meeting him. I, in turn, gave no

61

indication of my disappointment at the modesty of the supper presented, an offering of scrambled eggs on toast.

Eilin had been shy of Nancy's beauty and confidence during those early months in New York. She worked in the woolen section of a big department store where they sold a range of garments for men and women. She laughed when Nancy asked if she'd like to work in a department store too. Lord bless us, she knew she wasn't grand enough to work in one of those; indeed she was lucky to get that first job as a kitchen maid. Maisie had arranged it with their parish priest, Fr Fogarty, and she was to work for the O'Neills, a well-off Catholic family in Manhattan. Barely two days had passed before Mrs O'Neill told her she'd have to let her go, as she needed someone who knew how to clean and polish. There was never any call back home for the sort of cleaning and polishing they wanted, she told Maisie tearfully, so she could hardly be blamed for not knowing how to do it.

Mrs O'Neill was a kind enough woman and knew of a well-off neighbour, Mrs Rosenthal, who needed a scullery maid who could be trained. She recommended her for the job, and she'd been glad to get it despite the smaller wages. It left her with just enough to pay Maisie and Jack rent, and a little over. Mrs Rosenthal's housekeeper was called Sofia, and it was she who taught her how to polish and scrub. She made her do things over and over until she was satisfied that they were done right, and indeed she was grateful to her, as it had given her the training she needed to apply successfully for other jobs in domestic service.

Kate was to discover that Eilin's early life in New York could not have been easy. Like so many other young women from a similar background, she was ill fitted for her role in domestic service during those early years. She lacked experience and skills in the kind of homecare required, and her independent attitude and lack of servility were often mistaken for impudence.

How easy her life in Ireland had seemed by comparison. While, at home, she had to draw water from the well and help cook their simple meals, or brush out the floors in the morning and feed the animals and hens, but there was little else to do. Indeed, it was nothing like the amount and kind of work that was now expected of her. Sure they were mad about cleaning, and you had to clean their floors until they shone like their dishes. After many years of domestic service in America, she knew that she had eventually become a competent housekeeper, but she never liked the work. She was glad when those long years of washing, heating water in big boilers, scrubbing on a washboard and ironing with heavy flat irons that had to be separately heated, were at an end. Then there was the cooking on a coal stove that had to be fed, tended and cleaned in turn, and of course the sewing and darning with no electricity and only candles or gas lamps for light, and few mechanical aids. It left her with an abiding hatred of housework.

She had been with Mrs Rosenthal a year or so when the mistress asked her to go and fetch a pound of olives from the market. She didn't rightly know what they were, but Sofia described them and wrote the name down on a piece of paper to show to the stall holder. She had only been to the market once with Maisie and had found the crowds milling around, talking in different languages, very bewildering. The array of stalls and pushcarts selling all sorts of foods was astonishing, some she'd never heard of, like sauerkraut and pickles and different kinds of cheeses. She learnt from another

Irish woman that the strange meats she pointed to were called sausage. These were smoked and could be eaten without cooking them; some came from Poland, and some from Italy and Russia. There were stands selling fish, salted or smoked, as well as fresh, and it was good to be out, wandering around this colourful world. She was delighted to find the bearded man guarding an overflowing barrel of olives, and he obligingly made a container for her olives with a twist of brown paper. Stopping to watch a tall bony man trying to sell a gadget for peeling potatoes on the way back, she was nearly run down by a horse and cart and the driver shouted at her in some strange language.

Initially, she was not alarmed to find the mistress waiting for her, when she got back with the olives, though she could see that she was mad at something. When she got near, she started shouting at her, but she couldn't make out what she was saying. Sofia interrupted to say that the mistress wanted to know what had taken her so long. She hadn't thought she had done anything wrong and said that she was just looking at everything because the mistress hadn't told her she was in a hurry. Oh the Lord bless us, but she'd been angry then and told her that she was an insolent young woman and that she'd had enough of her. She was confused and couldn't see how she had been rude in answering truthfully the question she was asked. Sofia was always warning her about answering back, and she learnt that, as a maid, she was seen by her employer as an inferior person and that she should always be humble which was something she found difficult. Indeed, she knew that the Irish maids in America were generally thought to be too independent minded, and many of their employers hadn't liked that.

The sleet was surging noisily around her as she trudged back to Jack & Maisie's home. The shabby inhabitants of the lower Westside reeked of wet stale clothes, and she longed to join a trio of young people warming their hands around a chestnut brazier to put off having to relay the bad news. She glanced bleakly at the emaciated figure holding a placard with the words "Jesus Forgives" written on it. Sure there were people worse off, but she felt ashamed of having to go back and tell Maisie that she'd lost another job. She was very low then and knew that if she had the money she'd have gone back to Clare on the next boat.

"It's a pity we encouraged Annie to let her come out here," she overheard Maisie's sister Nora say not long after, "I can't see her ever making out." They were talking out on the fire escape that night, Nora, elbows on knees and chin cupped in her hands while Maisie sat and sewed. All the tenements had iron fire escapes running down the side of the buildings. The neighbours would sit out on them when the evenings were fine and often sleep there during the hot summer weather. Maisie just said, "God is good," and Eilin cried with loneliness in her room. God knows, it was a bleak time after this, trailing around agencies looking for work.

The chugging sound of the tug boats was homely as she wandered along by the Hudson. She'd been glad to get out of the tenement that morning. She'd noticed the ribbon of black crepe pinned to the door of her downstairs neighbour on her way out, and knew that their four-year-old little girl must have died of pneumonia she'd been diagnosed with a few days earlier. Three startled mallards flew low over the river which was beginning to flush under the rising sun. She soon got to know her neighbourhood on the lower Westside as she walked its miles of new wharves, passing the iron foundries, sawmills, stone and lumber yards all along the river. She knew that all of these provided work in warehousing, trucking, tugboat and rail employment for many of her countrymen and other immigrants. Both Jack and his son Johnny worked on the railroad, but Joe had secured a better paid post as a foreman at the Nabisco biscuit factory in Chelsea. He said that it was because it was a unionised establishment that conditions and benefits there were good. It also offered its workers paid overtime so that Joe, and his wife Aggie who did piece work there, seemed better off than most people in the area.

She became very used to the noisy rattle of the elevated train that rushed its carriages way above their heads, puffing and clattering along Ninth Avenue. It was great to catch a ride on this from the big station in the middle of the intersection at West Fourteenth Street, all the way uptown.

What was the name of that first department store she had visited? She had thought it a fairyland, with its beautiful wooden fittings and cushioned velvet seats, and of course all the materials, furniture, clothes, gadgets and jewellery; stuff you could only dream of. It was magic the way the electric lights would shine back at you out of the polished brass and gilded mirrors, but the Lord save us, she'd been frightened that first time she took a ride on the elevator. The rails of luxurious coats, costumes and dresses shimmered with colour as she passed on her way to the glass-topped counter where they sold the replaceable collars she needed. The wall behind this was lined with shelves and drawers of hosiery, collars, gloves and handkerchiefs.

What a relief it was when Maisie gave her a message from Jimmy, one of the foremen at the garment factory she worked for, to say that she was to go down the following morning at 8:30, as there might be a job going. She had hugged her; are you sure, she asked? Maisie was sure; she did piece work there, finishing off garments, and on asking about a vacancy was told they would give Eilin a start. Thanks be to God and his Blessed Mother, she'd be able to pay her way again. Down at the factory early next morning she was brought into a big room with high ceilings which she was surprised to find brightly lit with electric light. She knew that when Maisie did piecework on first coming to America, that she sat for hours, often late into the night, with just gaslight to work by. "At that time," she told Eilin, "you'd find women, a lot of Jewish and Italian women too, all over the Lower East Side, huddled in little rooms doing this poorly paid work."

The time went by slowly, sitting with the other girls at tables with rows of sewing machines, but at least the hours were fixed, and she had more time off. The girls too were friendly, and it was there that she met Maria, a Lithuanian Jewish girl, who would later die in a terrible fire that burnt down the factory. The shame of it was that the owners never unlocked the fire exit which they should have done, and those poor girls lost their lives because of that. There were lots of complaints about pay and conditions when she worked there, and there were threats of strike action too which the priests didn't like. Sure she hadn't paid much attention; she'd been so pleased to get the job and to be able to pay her way. Mind you, as time went by, you had to keep reminding herself that you were lucky, as you'd get weary with the monotony of it all, and there was no let-up. You couldn't take a break even if it was that time of the month and you didn't feel well. You were afraid that they'd give the job to someone else; there were always that many people looking for jobs.

The streets all around the factory were lively. You'd laugh sometimes listening to the street vendors shouting out their wares in German, Russian and Yiddish and she got to know the different languages and nationalities. It was hard not to laugh at the bushy beards, and especially the ringlets, that a lot of the Jewish men had, but Maria who was a very soft-hearted girl, got mad at her about that and told her it was rude and cruel. She thought that a lot of the Jewish boys were very pale maybe from too much praying, though she didn't think that their synagogues were anywhere near as grand as the Catholic Churches.

She never tired of wandering around the markets; the Gansevoort market sold mostly fruit and vegetables, and the West Washington one had meat, poultry, milk, cheese and the like. At first, she couldn't believe her eyes on seeing the quantity of fruit and vegetables everywhere and thought that it was just as well that there were all the thousands of people around to eat them. There were fruits like melons and pineapples, the likes of which she had never seen in West Clare, and vegetables she'd never even heard of like zucchini and eggplant. You could look forever at the mounds of meat, game and fowls and the tanks of fish, as well as the piles of shellfish, crabs, oysters and lobsters.

The buzz of life in the streets of the Lower West Side and the banter that went on would keep you entertained. It was grand, too, when a cousin or friend would buy you a meal in one of the cheap eating houses in the area. You could watch the children playing in the playgrounds of Chelsea and Hudson parks, and it was a wonder to see so many little boys diving off Gansevoort St pier and swimming in the Hudson, in spite of it being so near the sanitation pier. It was even more of a wonder that so few of them seemed to become ill in spite of it being terrible unhealthy. She recalled the lean cadaverous face of a man staring into his drink through the windows of a saloon; shadows cast by the flickering gas light played across his unhappiness. Later through another saloon window she caught sight of the silhouettes of dancers and an inward looking accordionist playing in the corner and felt happier. The Irish were surely great drinkers, and it was them that kept all the saloons and licensed premises in the area in business. They were nearly all owned by Irishmen too, Shannon's, O'Neill's, and the Blarney Rose, where she used to join Maisie and Jack after Mass on Sunday when they met up with the rest of the family there.

There would often be singing. She remembered being reduced to tears when Johnny McElligot's fine voice rang out with the sad words of Tom Moore's melody after a bottle or two of porter on those Sunday mornings.

Sweet vale of Avoca! How calm could I rest
In thy bosom of shade, with the friends I love best
Where the storms that we feel in this cold world should cease
And our hearts, like thy waters, be mingled in peace

Any social life they had took place in and around the parish Church of St Veronica's. Joe was very proud of having been an altar boy there and, like all the other first or second generation Irish, was educated at the parish school alongside his brother and sister. There they learnt step-dancing and popular music hall songs and of course Moore's melodies; everyone loved them.

She used to go to early morning Mass back then; you'd feel less lonely being with so many Irish folk. It was always crowded with many of the working men catching it before going to work. Jack told her that seven o'clock

Anne Loughnane

Mass at St Veronica's would be full of longshoremen who would be on the piers by eight o'clock. Nearly all the longshoremen were Irish, but she learnt that the wages earned were very low and families often needed the additional earnings of women to survive. At St Bernard's Church, down a block from the meat market, the early morning weekday Mass would be full of butchers just off the third shift, and still in their white coats bloodied red from their work. She enjoyed many the dance and picnic organised by one parish committee or another, over her years in New York.

Reflecting on how reliant the Irish were on the church to care for their needs back then, I wondered how they'd have fared without it. I was a little uneasy about my own professional role being colonised by the church, aware as I was of its controlling legacy during the previous decades in Ireland. The ridiculous levels of censorship it exercised over freedom of expression might now be a laughing matter, but it had not been so for the many writers forced to leave the country in order to express themselves and make a living. I also knew that while claiming to be the sole provider of services for the poor and those on the margins of society, the quality of the mercy extended was sometimes bleak indeed, as had been the case for many unmarried mothers and their children. Their efforts to outlaw music and house dances in the poor depressed Ireland of the Thirties and Forties reflected a joyless faith that I wanted no part of, yet the substantial pockets of goodness and generosity which I had experienced all my life had been fuelled by a very real faith which I cherished.

CHAPTER 9

New Experiences

Most sustaining of all for me were the strong working relationships forged with a range of community-minded individuals. For the most part, these were people who gave their service voluntarily with a generosity and warmth I found humbling.

Paddy and Bridie McGarry lived in a long row of bedraggled cottages, in what was the poorest section of the town. The front garden at number twelve in striking contrast to the jumbled chaos of its neighbours, comprised a long narrow strip pleated with orderly drills of potatoes, carrots, parsnips, onions and turnips. In summer, there would be lettuce, tomatoes, strawberries and bushes of blackcurrants and raspberries. I knew that this was Paddy's domain. He was a quiet man who seldom said much and usually sat by the Raeburn stove smoking his pipe when I visited. He had the restful quality of someone very at ease in his own body and home.

Maisie, with her ready laughter and genuine warmth, was a comfort to Eilin during her early years in New York. She and Nancy became solid friends later on, but she had been shy of her back then. Nancy, with her black hair and tall slender form, was beautiful, and though she made all her own clothes, she looked just like gentry. It was great to get her cast-offs which were a lot better than her own clothes. Nancy was going out with a young man from Tipperary called Matty Doyle. He was a longshoreman then but had applied to become a fireman as there were a lot of Irishmen in the fire service. You'd get more money for that and besides it was a secure job, and sure they were delighted when the letter came saying that he was successful. They used to bring her with them to parish dances, but she knew that she'd have to find her own friends, and that was when she thought of Peig. Searching out her address, she set out for O'Meara's Tavern on her day off. It was easy to find, and there was Peig working away behind the bar and glad to see her. She didn't know why she cried then; it was a strange thing to do because she had been so happy to find her.

Oh, they had a great talk. Peig wanted to know everything that had happened since the boat, and it all poured out. She told her about the job and Maisie and Nancy and Matty Doyle, and Peig asked if anyone had broken her heart yet. Sure, where would she meet anyone who'd break her heart, and she working all her days. "Haven't you a day off, and aren't there the parish dances, and there's Coney Island and lots of places to go," said Peig. She told her that she didn't like to be always hanging off the coat tails of Nancy and Matty, and she didn't know anyone else to do things with. Peig was quiet for a bit before asking when she was next off, saying that she'd try and get that day off too so that they could take a trip out to Coney Island together.

Those first years in New York could be very lonely, and many's the night she cried herself to sleep, but having a friend like Peig was great. She was a real devil-may-care creature and great fun to be with. Their first trip to Coney Island was spent gawking at everything, the hawkers, the teeming crowds, the musicians and the colours and flashing lights of the shows and rides. They were heady with the excitement of it all, and Peig said that it was like a huge box of fireworks going off. She could still remember the thrill of the roller coaster and Ferris wheel rides, and the delight of the chicken carousel; its name always made them laugh. This had thirty-eight chickens and fourteen ostriches instead of horses. Nothing however, could beat the steeplechase ride for excitement. It took place on elevated parallel mechanical race tracks, with horses that plunged wildly across a tiny lake, before rushing down through a tunnel, and finally racing over loads of dips and hurdles to the finishing line. Then at the end, you had to leave through what was called a comedy lane, where a machine with air would blow the men's hats off and send the women's dresses whishing upwards. It was comical to see the expressions on folk's faces and these would always have you in stitches.

It was on one of her trips to Coney Island that she met Josh. She and Peig pushed their way through the crowds to get a place under the sun canopy on the steamboat. It was so hot that they were very glad of the breeze from the river as they passed the resorts of Rockaway and Brighton beach to reach Coney Island by noon. Peig found two bathing suits that more or less fitted them and they went straight to the women's lockers to change. She'd never worn one of these before, and to tell the truth she felt a bit naked in it, but Peig just laughed pulling her out of the locker, and they ran down to the waves. They had a grand time playing like children in the lovely cool of the water. The sensation of the sand slipping away under her and the wavelets washing over her legs was gorgeous, as they sat at the water's edge. Never having learnt to swim, they had to content themselves with paddling and splashing about; none of her people swam because they believed you were more likely to drown if you could swim. There were seagulls all around, gobbling bits of leftover rolls and hot dogs. These were different than the ones at home, not so clean or scary looking. They were a sort of smudged, brownish colour and seemed smaller and homelier.

Later on towards evening, they idled along the pier watching the men fishing, in twos and threes. They spoke in different languages but seemed comradely with each other, and some of them had bits of old rope or thick twine they used with a hook at the end. Suddenly a line swung back slapping a reddish winged fish at their feet. It was a robin fish, one of the men told them, which she thought a good name for the plump russet little creature. She didn't like the way they left it flapping its life out on the pier and asked one of the men why they didn't kill it, but he just shrugged. It was when they were eating a hot dog from one of the stalls that a dark-haired young man, leaning on the counter of the shooting gallery, called to them "come and have a go", but Peig said that they were all out of money. She knew that he was taken by Peig's merry eyes when he offered them a free shot and lined up the rifles so that they each had a turn. He was due to be replaced in an hour and asked if they'd come back then and he'd show them around. She was mortified when Peig said that she couldn't, because she had to be back in the Tavern for work but that Eilin would. Poor Josh, for that was his name, didn't know what to say, and she could see that he was trying to pretend that he wasn't disappointed. She knew that he had a kind heart when he smiled and said, "Great, see you then."

She was a thin and wispy girl back then, not much to look at, with sandy hair and freckles and people didn't notice her. She wasn't even hurt when she overheard

74

Nora saying to Maisie one night "It's not as if she's anything to look at, so we can hardly hope for a romance." She'd heard it many times before from when she was a child. She'd never had a boyfriend since Mikey, who hardly counted as a proper one, and she didn't want to go back and meet Josh that night, but Peig pushed her into it. "He's not going to eat you Eilin, can't you just go and walk with him for half an hour, sure wasn't he decent enough giving us free shots and he'd be offended if you didn't turn up." She knew that Peig, God rest her soul, was trying to help her along socially for she was very backward at that time.

Well, she did go back and found Josh cheerfully waiting for her. He was a bit on the small side, but strong and sturdy and with a kind of puckered monkey face and shy dark eyes. They walked along the shore listening to the whispering sounds of the tufted sea grass and the hiss of the rolling surf. He picked up a cockle shell, marvelling at its spiral, and they both liked the delicate patterns left by the spume on the edge of the beach. He spoke with a strange accent which she sometimes found hard to make out, but she liked the quiet way he listened to you. Peig thought he was ugly, but she was so tall and handsome herself that she only had eyes for tall good looking fellows. Eilin was surprised to find that she liked him, and smiled when he told her that there were as many stars in the sky as there were grains of sand, but she didn't think that could be true.

Josh was from a village called Callington in Cornwall, and his family were all miners on his father's side and fisher-folk on his mother's. His world was so different to hers, and she listened with interest to the stories he told her about the tin mines that used to be in that area. It was because these had closed down in recent years and there was no longer any work for them in Cornwall that two of his uncles had gone to Montana. There was a lot of mining there at that time, and their skills were needed. He said that it paid well but was very dangerous work, and one of his uncles had been killed by a collapsing mine shaft along with many other miners. His other uncle bought land and horses with the money he made and was building up a ranch out there. He it was who'd paid for Josh's ticket out, as he wanted him to come and work on the ranch. Josh's job on Coney Island was just for the summer, his uncle would be coming into New York sometime in early October to collect supplies, and he would return with him.

She went down to Coney Island as often as she could that summer. She was dazzled by the excitement of it all, but she knew that more than anything, she wanted to be with Josh. She hadn't been lonely since she met him and was surprised that she was able to talk more freely to him than to her own people. They were a bit shy, and maybe excited at first, when they found out that they had different religions. She was shocked when Josh told her he was a Methodist and remembered saying, "sure that's just another kind of a black Protestant," and he grinned and said that he'd rather be a black Protestant than one of them superstitious Catholics who believed in all sorts of magic. It wasn't long before this became something they teased each other about, enjoying the intimate strangeness of it all. It was so easy to talk to him, and she marvelled at how free she felt when with him.

It was strange to discover that his uncle had worked alongside a number of Irish miners from Cork. These men had developed their mining skills in the Allihies copper mines there, and like his uncle, went to Montana looking for jobs when they closed. Josh told her that his uncle thought well of the Irish miners and became close friends with one of them, Jim Murphy, who began homesteading alongside him. When she asked if he knew anything about farming, he was a bit put out and told her that he knew all about horses. Their cottage in Cornwall had looked out over Bodmin moor on the one side and Dartmoor on the other, and he had grown up catching and riding the wild ponies on Dartmoor. His uncle Jack was planning on training and breaking horses which, he said, he'd be well able to help him with.

She loved the stories he told her of Cornish life and its legends and remembered the one about a warrior called Drem, one of Arthur's war-band, who, from a tor on the moor near where Josh had lived, could see a gnat as far away as Scotland. There was another one about a warrior called Medyr who could see through the legs of a wren over in Ireland. It was strange to learn that they also had holy wells in Cornwall, and he talked about one called St Sampson's near where he lived. Her heart was in her mouth when he told her stories about smuggling and the dare-devil things the smugglers got up to, but she was truly shocked by his fearful stories about the wreckers. To think that they'd lure men to their death just to plunder their wealth was a terrible thing. No matter how poor they were, sure it would have been better to die than to do the like of that. She remembered her father's account of the plundering that went on after the wreck of the Edmond in Kilkee Bay in November of 1850 when his own relatives had been among the survivors. The local people plundered whatever they could lay their hands on, even stripping the clothes from the dead bodies; she'd heard that some of the survivors had to beg for their own clothes back to cover their nakedness. That was bad but sure the poor folk were near death from starvation themselves. Paidi told her that Fr. Comyn, the parish priest in Kilkee at the time, made the people give back a lot of the plundered property. It wasn't like in Josh's stories; they hadn't caused the wreck to happen.

When I asked Eilin if she'd fallen in love with Josh, she replied, "Sure we didn't have any of that kind of talk then child, but I liked being with him and I knew 'twas the same for him."

Eilin recalled that evening later on in the summer when he asked her to lie with him. She was upset then because she wanted to do so, sure they were young, and it was natural that they'd want to, but she told him that she couldn't because she was afraid she might have a baby and that would be the end of her. He didn't try to force her or anything, but she knew he was disappointed, and she thought that maybe he wouldn't want to see her again after that. When she asked him that night, he looked surprised and said that he wanted to see her as much as he could until he had to go away. It made her want to lie with him all the more but sure what could she do? Maybe there'd be ways now but those were innocent times, and they were very ignorant about a lot of things.

I asked her if she'd written to him when he went to Montana, but she said no, that she didn't think that he could write and hadn't wanted to embarrass him by asking. She also told me that she knew their worlds were too different for them to marry and that it was better to let it end naturally. I was curious and tried to find out if she'd missed him. I can still recall Eilin's response: "Well child, I asked him the very same question, would he miss me, and his reply brought me great contentment. He said that he didn't know, but that he thought that he would think of me every day of his life."

I had been moved by Eilín's account of this significant interlude in her life and wondered if my own hunger for love could have been as simply assuaged. I thought about the attractive American whom I had met in London and whose current correspondence augured a deeper interest in pursuing the relationship. Reflecting on my confused feelings, and knowing myself at risk of letting hope distort my perceptions, I shoved on the most recent tape he'd sent as I drove back.

Roberta Flack's wonderful voice rang out …

> *The first time ever I saw your face*
> *I thought the sun rose in your eyes*
> *And the moon and the stars*
> *Were the gifts you gave*

How I wished…

CHAPTER 10

The Church, Dancing and Paddy Sullivan

I could appreciate how the faith of those thousands of emigrants had cushioned their often frightened souls from the full impact of the loneliness, poverty and hostility which had greeted so many of them during those harsh early years. While no doubt there was an element of establishing and sustaining a power base in the New World, I was inclined to think that the church's commitment to addressing the educational, health and social needs of the people reflected also a deep humanity, supported by a robust spiritual life. To those people, their faith was undoubtedly a major source of their confidence in themselves and their future. Aware of the reduced certainty and ambivalence characterising my own faith, I was yet in thrall to the good it could generate.

Sunday Mass was at the heart of their week, it was there Eilin met up with neighbours, cousins and friends met through parish dances and fairs. There were other societies that organised events; some of the names she could remember, the Clan Na Gael and the Ancient Order of Hibernians, but she didn't have much to do with these. She knew that Peig was a member of the Gaelic League and was surprised to find her so passionate about anything to do with the language, as she was usually so casual. She would drag her along to some of the feiseanna and make her sit for hours listening to old *sean-nos* singers and to poetry recitals in Gaelic. Peig was nervous the year she herself entered for the singing competition, though she was a lovely singer with beautiful Irish, and came second. She herself found too much of the singing a bit dreary, all the songs seemed so miserable, but she loved to watch the step-dancing and was transfixed by Tommy Hall, who'd not long arrived from Ireland. He won first prize for every dancing event he entered, and he'd gone on to found one of New York's most famous schools for teaching Irish dancing.

After a couple of years of factory work, Eilin decided to try again for a post in service. Maisie was hoping that Nancy and Matty could live with her when they got married, in order to save a little money before they looked for a place of their own. It would be easier for them if Eilin had a home somewhere else, and a job in service would give her food and shelter. Also, it usually paid better than factory work, which would let her start to save some money. By then she had set her heart on going home, even if it was just for a holiday and she was determined to save for this.

Well, didn't she get a job with the English family in Brooklyn, who employed Maisie's friend, Mary O'Brien, as cook. There were four children in the family, and she thought that this might make it a more homely place to be. It soon became clear that this was not her home and that she was there only to work. In the beginning, she used to try to talk to Mrs Ashe when she came into the kitchen, but she would just tell her sharply to get on with her work. Mary told her that she should only speak if the mistress spoke to her first and that it was very important that she should know her place. She didn't rightly know what this meant at the time, but Mary explained that the people you worked for were only interested in the work you did for them and thought you were being rude if you tried to talk to them about anything else. She thought this strange and unfriendly, but she got used to it. After a while, you could see that they didn't even notice that you were in the same room; it was as if you were invisible.

She was lucky to have the company of Mary, and the pair of them shared a tiny room. She was a good humoured kindly soul and a great comfort to her. It could be very lonely, and you'd often get to feel isolated from everyone when working in service. A lot of the families knew they needed you but wished that they didn't, and you didn't feel you belonged.

The kitchen where she and Mary spent most of their time and ate their meals was a dark, airless room. In the summer, it was full of the smells of rotten food and the garbage, which was stacked just outside the windows. It used to be cosy enough in winter when the range was lighting, not that they had much time to enjoy their ease by it. They were up by six a.m. and had to have the range and fires lit, the rooms dusted and made ready for breakfast, and the front hall and steps brushed and cleared before the family was down. Then she would rush upstairs to get the two youngest children, Dan and Jack aged five and seven, ready for school, and deal with their reluctance and tantrums. She recalled the weekly round of jobs; Monday: clothes-washing, including sheets towels, tablecloths etc; Tuesday, ironing; Wednesday, upstairs cleaning; Thursday, downstairs cleaning; Friday, polishing the silver and cleaning the bathrooms and Saturday, baking. There was also the spring-cleaning and lots of other jobs whenever the mistress took a notion that something needed doing.

You couldn't call your soul your own unless you were away from the house.

She would grab at any chance to escape and was always delighted when she was sent to the Fulton fish market on the East Side waterfront. It was great to walk under the mighty suspended span of the Brooklyn Bridge, built, as she well knew, by Irish labour. It was said to be about a hundred feet in height and soared over the entrance to the east river. She knew that it was held up by steel cables, but still wondered how an airy graceful arc the like of that could possibly hold up such a gigantic bridge. Jack told her that the whole of South Port, which she could see from the bridge, used to be heaving with great-masted sailing ships as far as the eye could see. She knew that he lamented the arrival of the ocean going steam ships replacing the romantic clippers, as they required the deeper waters of the Hudson on the West Side, and the East Side wharves fell into relative disuse. She thought that they still looked busy enough now.

The whiff of seaweed as she glanced down at the gulls swirling in the slipstream of the barges reminded her of home. The barges poked their way between the ageing cargo ships and the coastal steamers that ferried passengers to Brooklyn beach and the port towns of New England. There were two men naked to the waist helping tie up one of the smaller trawling schooners which delivered fish to the market, and one of them had a coiled serpent in lurid reds and greens tattooed on his back. There was a whole fleet of these schooners unloading big creels of fresh fish, crabs, lobsters and all kinds of sea creatures she didn't even recognise. The fishermen told her that they would be taken straight to the market to be auctioned. She hurried by a drunk man howling in the filth of the streets around the wharves where there were a lot of men, and some women too, drinking, and the morning still early. The huge earth-coloured building housing the fish market rang with the racket of fishmongers and the cries of the auctioneers and their runners. She made her way through the jostle of buyers, all out for bargains, to the oyster stand already surrounded by customers.

She knew that a lot of her friends were worse off than her, particularly if you were the only servant in a large family. You'd be expected to do not only the usual cleaning, and scrubbing and laundry work, but also to cook and serve all the meals, answer the door and the mistress's bell. They couldn't stick it sometimes and would leave to find a better job. There was a lot of turnover in domestic service that time. The women would try to find easier jobs in bigger houses where there were lots of staff to share the load. She worked for a short time herself as a kitchen maid in a big, beautiful house on Fifth Avenue where there were seven staff caring for two people, the master, mistress and her little poodle. There, it was the upper servants, the butler and footmen, who expected you to be humble and the master and mistress seemed a bit more human. She did not stay long as her duties, scrubbing all the passages to the kitchen, laundry and staff dining room, as well as helping the cook and the assistant cook, all took place one floor underground. She found she was becoming run down without any sunlight or fresh air, and besides, she had been offered the post which she was to hold for the next eight years.

She had begun to save some money by this time and remembered the excitement with which she opened an account with the Emigrant Industrial Savings Bank. This was a major step toward making her way back to Ireland, and it was a beacon of hope for her. On her way there she dodged the children playing games of statues and point ball and narrowly avoided collision with one little boy careering down a sloping side street on what they called a pusho, a kind of homemade scooter made from broken roller skates. While wondering if she'd have time to take the trolley to the Irish Industries depot on West 23 rd Street, where she had seen a lovely Connemara marble pendant, she unexpectedly met Peig. They both stood for a while with the crowd who had gathered nearby, to cheer a group of volunteers marching away to the war in Europe. Peig had a copy of the *Irish Advocate* with her, and pointed to an advertisement for a dance in Donovan's Hall the following Thursday; they agreed to meet up and go.

The dances were the highlight of their week at that time, and there were dance halls flourishing all over New York, especially in Manhattan, as well as the impromptu dances which sprang up in the back rooms of taverns. There were lots of Irish musicians playing then, not only the old tunes, but modern ones as well, from whatever shows were on, and she'd danced to many of them. A lot of the Irish acted and played music in the vaudeville theatre too, and she still remembered musicians such as James Morrison, Michael Coleman and Tom Ennis. The church got a bit incensed about them at times, as a lot of the Protestant churches, particularly the Methodists, thought that they were leading young people into immoral ways. In 1913, after the tango, which they said came from the bawdy houses of Buenos Aires, became popular, Cardinal Farley forbade the ladies auxiliary committee of St Vincent's Hospital to hold any dances at their annual fundraising event. She remembered how mad Norah, who was a member of this committee, had been. "How on God's earth does he expect us to raise $5000 without a dance," she snapped at Maisie, as this was always the main fundraising event. Finally in1916, the church put a ban on dancing in any parish gatherings.

It hadn't bothered herself or Peig, it just meant that they went to Tighe's or Donovan's, the kind of commercial dance halls that sprouted everywhere as a result of the ban. Sure they were delighted because of course the ban removed their competition. The priests began to change their tune when they saw that it didn't stop the dancing, and they were losing a lot of money. It wasn't long before the parish dancing began to come back. She used to hate it if she missed what they called the maid's dance on Thursday night which, as was the case for most women in domestic service, was her only night off. It was great to meet up with the other Irish girls who worked as maids, and the chatting would be a comfort. Each week they'd look through the *Irish Advocate* and the other Irish weekly newspapers which carried advertisements for all the dances, to see what was on.

Peig and herself would sometimes attend those run by the Kerry and Claremen's associations. Here they'd meet people with whom they'd have a connection, and it felt homely. You'd sometimes see some of the poor lonely souls not long arrived, crying with the relief of meeting someone from their home county, as dances run by the Irish county associations were always popular with recently arrived immigrants. It was surely a great comfort to meet old friends and neighbours in the big city. A great favourite with Peig and herself was Donovan's Hall at Columbus Circle. This was a large Irish dance hall which opened in 1906 and Mr Donovan himself taught them how to waltz and do the quickstep because these were dances new to them. He often taught in the dancing classes which he advertised and told them that he'd taught more people to dance than all the other schools combined.

There were always loads of men who wanted to dance with Peig, even though she'd often tell them what she thought of them and it wouldn't be complimentary . Sometimes she'd just laugh at them and tell them that she wasn't that desperate yet, which wasn't very nice but you had to laugh. Sure, it was because she was full of fun that they liked to be around her. It was at a Claremen's association dance that Eilin ran into Paddy Sullivan from Kilrush. She was so delighted to see him that she forgot her shyness when he swung her around into a big hug. It wasn't him, but his friend, another Kilrush man called John Walshe, that Peig and herself fell for that night. He was a tall fireman and very handsome in his navy blue uniform and polished shoes, and you could see that he kept himself very fit.

She couldn't remember why they started talking about evictions, but his stories about the bailiff's men tearing down the houses during the Vandeleur evictions, so that the people couldn't creep back into them at night time, upset her. She knew that these took place two years before she was born in 1888, but his account brought back fearful images. He had just been five then. John Walshe became a hero to her when, some years later, he was the fireman who rescued Ida Goldberg, a young girl who was trapped in the upper floor of a blazing building. There was a big award ceremony for him in the City Halls, and they were very proud of him. It was a long time after that when she met him at a bazaar in the Sacred Heart Church in Highbridge. She never forgot it, because he and his wife brought her for a spin around the block in the first motor car she was ever in. She remembered that it was a model-A Ford.

However, it was not John but Paddy who was to become important to her over the next few years. She supposed it was because, being timid, she liked it that he was so sure of himself. She ignored Peig's comments about never having seen anyone lower a pint of porter in less time than Paddy.

I thought about Peig whose zest for life and indomitable spirit, had, I knew, been a lifeline for Eilin during her lonely years in New York. I wondered if her years of servitude had engendered that wariness I sensed in her, or was it the fruit of decades of poverty and helplessness. I reflected on the very different trajectories of Eilin's life and that of Bridie McGarry: both had similar legacies of famine and hardship in their backgrounds, but Bridie had emerged confident, generous and forward looking while Eilin still seemed trapped within an older, fearful world of helplessness.

The sky was threatening as I made my way back to the car. The air carried the scent of turf smoke and rain, the loamy smell of my year in West Clare. Lost in my thoughts, I noticed that the collie up ahead, waiting with relish to launch an assault on the long-suffering Morris Minor, had different coloured eyes. Blasé by this time and well aware that there was no fear of the dog doing himself an injury, I paid little attention, smiling at the startled rush of little birds that always preceded the attack.

CHAPTER 11

Politics, Fun and Broadway

"Come in Anne." The stocky, lame figure encased in an old-fashioned wraparound floral apron exuded warmth and welcome. Bridie had one short leg, whether from birth or polio, I couldn't recall, and indeed, neither Bridie or anyone else paid attention to this. "I have a great pot of soup all ready so sit yourself down," she said, and I basked in the warmth of this motherly woman and her welcoming home. This was not only a refuge for me; it was the comfort of Bridie's whole community. While nobody's fool, it was to her that the waifs and strays of the town, and particularly of that mean row of cottages, came when in trouble.

There was a welcome for the young girl with an unwanted pregnancy, the victims of domestic abuse and the many with financial or alcohol-fuelled problems, but it was her kindly tolerance for those who could only be described as feckless that I most admired. "I don't know how you do it," I said one day, as Bridie, yet again, went down to visit a particular family whose ongoing drinking bouts, followed by empty expressions of remorse were the bane of my professional life. "Sure they never learnt different when they were children," she said simply, "and that's harder to learn when you're older." She and Paddy were rightly proud of the achievements of their three children who had all gone to college or university, but had no wish to move up in the world themselves. I admired the responsibility they shouldered for their community and their fierce loyalty to it. I knew that their humanity was fuelled by a deep piety. They led the sort of prayerful life that had characterised my own childhood, but which was already dying out then in Ireland, and many's the night I'd be invited to say the rosary with them before leaving.

Speaking of this with my friend Maggie O'Dea one evening, I recalled the longing in Maggie's voice: "I wish I could have faith but I've never been able to, I prayed for it, but if there's a God there, he didn't hear me." I was curious, having seen her at Mass on Sunday and asked why she wanted to have faith. "I think it must be a great comfort," Maggie said, adding that she liked to go to Mass because she was hoping that maybe some day the faith would rub off on her, and she smiled rather self-mockingly. I sensed a loneliness behind her words and, liking her, felt a little sad. Indeed, I worried about my own *a la carte* approach to my faith and sometimes wondered idly if I'd be excommunicated, if the powers that be really knew what I thought about a number of things.

Eilin was surprised to discover that Paddy was interested in politics and was in the thick of the electioneering fever that carried Big Tim Sullivan into office in the 1909 election. They said that he was born of Irish parents in the squalor and poverty of the Hudson River tenements. She knew that he was a hugely successful Tammany Hall boss and that everyone in the lower Manhattan area had been loyal to him for a long time now. She was surprised to hear that not only the Irish but also the Jews, Germans and Italians supported him. Paddy told her that he worked closely with all these different peoples of the Bowery and that he chose his captains from among them. It was Big Tim who got Maisie's son Johnny taken on at the railroad depot when he was in despair, poor soul, after five months of unemployment. They believed that Big Tim would look after their interests, and surely that was a good thing when you felt that a lot of people were against you. Nobody paid any attention when they said that he used to take bribes, nor to any of the other accusations of corruption. They just knew that he could be trusted to look after them

It was a regular thing in those days for the men interested in politics to gather in a back room of one of the saloons. They used to play a game called pinochle and would talk and plan politics into the small hours while playing for drinks or money. She knew that Paddy went regularly to their meetings in O'Meara's Tavern where Peig worked. She heard that he had become one of Big Tim's right-hand men, and indeed there was no doubting his admiration for him. She got to be a bit worried as she kept hearing that Big Tim was little better than a crook. She didn't want to believe this, but some of the stories she heard didn't give the lie to it either. She remembered Jack telling Maisie one evening, that a few of his friends who went to a cockfight organised by the Long Island branch of the party had been busted. All those present were placed under arrest, except for Judge Delahanty who managed to escape. Wasn't he then found at a friend's house where he had to hear the applications for bail from his companions of a short while before, which of course he had to accept. The culprits were all brought before him to be judged the following morning and he fined each one $10 and told them that if they trespassed again, they would go to prison. It made you laugh, but still, she didn't want Paddy to get into trouble.

She had been flabbergasted some years later when she discovered that her employer, Mrs Rodensky and her feisty elderly mother were loyal supporters of Big Tim because of his support for the vote for women. She couldn't be bothered herself with the whole women's suffrage movement, it seemed a waste of time. She and the other Irish women thought it was mostly about divorce, abortion and birth control and that it was being organised by the Protestant women against the Irish and the Catholics. Later on, she had to admit that she did wonder; by then she had begun to think for herself more, and she would go on to support trade unionism and education for girls as well as higher education for women, even when the priests were against it. She had learnt that only by these means could poor people and women gain any rights.

Neither she nor Peig had much interest in politics, but they had a lot of fun with Paddy and his friends. With them around, they had a gay old time and were never short of dance partners. At the parish fairs there would be portable tables set up with lots of delicious things to eat; cooked hams or all kind of bolognas if there was an Italian community and cakes donated by the parish. There would be crowds of young ones around the red lemonade stand where the women attendants would have a job trying to keep them from falling into the tubs. They'd always make Paddy and the boys enter for the athletic games and the tug of war and, of course, the "catch the greasy pig" event. Her great delight was the music and dancing and, with Paddy in tow, she was guaranteed to have a great time for he was a wonderful dancer. Sometimes the others would leave off dancing themselves and stand back just to watch them, especially when they did the Clare set, as not many knew how to do this.

Paddy was a great favourite with Maisie and Nora, which surprised her because Nora never liked Peig, and

Paddy was just as wild. She heard Nora say to Maisie one day that it was a pity she had taken up with Peig, "as she'll not better herself with her," but Maisie replied, "Sure what's the harm, isn't it nice for the child to have someone to go about with and I have to say that she makes me laugh with the things she comes out with." "That's just it," said Nancy, "she's so brazen and common, and the way she carries on with men is a scandal." Eilin hadn't cared too much, she liked Peig, and they used to have great laughs; all the same she was glad that Maisie stood up for her.

Nora was very different to Maisie, and to tell the truth, Eilin had been a little afraid of her. She was a big bosomed woman with slim hips and legs, whose black hair was dyed, and who always wore lipstick. They said that she was gorgeous looking when she was young, and Peig found out that she had been great for a long time with a well-known politician whose parents were Irish, but that he dropped her for a well-off American girl when he won office. After that, she went to night school to get herself educated and secured a clerical job with the local branch of the Democratic Party. All the time Eilin knew her; she was very religious and seemed to spend most of her time around the church when she wasn't working.

It was, however, Nora who would sometimes bring her to shows or concerts on Broadway and these were surely wonderful. She could still recall the excitement of the evening she was taken to hear the legendary John McCormack singing arias from the great operas. She had cried when he sang *Kathleen Mavourneen*, and *Danny Boy* for an encore; sure even Nora was in tears. They went to see the play called *The Colleen Bawn* by someone with a strange name, Dion Boucicault and was stunned to discover that it was based on a true story about a young girl from her own county of Clare. Decades later songs like *When Irish Eyes are Smiling* or *My Wild Irish Rose* could always transport her back to that time; to the buzz and glamour of Broadway.

It was a memorable night when, accompanying a friend of Norah's home after a show, they passed the crumpled figure of an old man in a doorway near the celebrated Shanley restaurant on 43rd Street where all the rich and famous went. He seemed to be lilting a music hall tune and raised his hand in feeble salute, pointing up to the full moon with an aureole around it like a halo. Shanley's was owned by a Leitrim family who employed a lot of the Irish, and that night the doorman, who was known to Nora's friend, let them have a quick peep inside. They stared in wonder at the crystal chandeliers and gilt furniture, and Nora pointed to what she called the champagne silk curtains, but when John McCormack himself smiled as he passed them on his way in, they knew that they'd never forget that evening.

It was during Eilin's final year in New York that Nora got tickets for her and Nancy for the opera. They wore their best dresses that night, and she thought they looked very smart until they caught sight of the elegant men and women in evening dress as they approached the big square-faced Metropolitan Opera House. Sure they were in another league altogether, but they hadn't minded and gazed in awe at the palatial hall with its mighty chandelier and massive gold damask curtain hung across the stage. She knew that they were in the cheaper seats as the folk all around them seemed more ordinary, like themselves. The story, called *Aida*, was about a princess and a captured slave and was by an Italian composer called Verdi. They were still bewitched by the splendour of the sun-drenched scenes on stage and the grandeur of the music when they spilled out onto the streets afterwards. A forest of black umbrellas fairly mushroomed around them as a squall of wind and rain swept in from the Atlantic. Having no umbrellas they got very wet walking home but, still in thrall to the glorious tenor voice of the hero, they hardly noticed.

I was well aware that Clare was a heartland of traditional music, but had been very surprised to learn from Maggie O'Dea that West Clare was also full of opera and light opera lovers and that whenever a touring opera company came to Ennis a bus would be hired to take folk there and back. However, when Eilín told me that she had been to the Metropolitan Opera House in New York, I stared in astonishment at the little old begrimed creature poking the fire and grinning at my disbelief.

I looked forward to surprising Tony and Karen with this unlikely story. This free-spirited couple, whose friendship eased my loneliness that year on the western seaboard, lived down on the wild Atlantic peninsula of Loophead. Tony was a potter, sculptor, musician and activist. I can still recall his narrow face full of vitality and humour as we discussed his plans to start a tin whistle class for the local children. I loved the distinctive pottery plaques he made of some of the neighbouring characters, and of the life around them, cutting turf, making hay etc. I purchased one that was to accompany me through many house moves. Karen was a dark, peaceful, and I thought, beautiful woman. She was a wonderful gardener and grew an array of vegetables, some very exotic for West Clare, at that time. I loved the interludes I shared with them in their attractive little cottage. The glow from the turf fire would cast flickering lights on the flagstone floor, and there were always fresh wildflowers on the table. It was very peaceful there.

CHAPTER 12

At Home in New York

The little fecker, that was definitely a bite ... I whipped back the bedclothes and, sure enough, there was the gleeful little bloodsucker hopping around the bed, chock full of my blood. I waited for the pause before its next jump, then grabbed the flea between thumb and forefinger, squeezing it tight while I ran the tap water over it. I was told that they lodged in the turf stacks by the fire, awaiting the arrival of succulent fresh blood donors, and it was putting me right off the peat fires I loved so much. I found it hard to get back to sleep and thought about the meeting I'd attended earlier in the community hall out on the tip of the Loophead peninsula. There, I'd spoken with local people about the need for a meals-on-wheels service. This would help some of the elderly isolated folk in the area who were struggling to care for themselves. I had been slightly embarrassed by Fr Duggan's rather fulsome introduction: "We are very lucky indeed to have the services of so able a professional... and I most strongly urge you to give her your full support. " I reflected wryly on how different professional life in West Clare was to that of the London inner city social service department where I had worked the previous year, and where such a quasi-feudal call for support was very unlikely.

Eilin went to work for the Rodensky family when the Rosenthals moved to California to be near their eldest daughter. This was to be her happiest experience of domestic service, and she would remain in contact with the two daughters of this family for the rest of her life.

Their cook, Willa, came of German stock, but the mistress herself presided over the cooking, and she was amazed to see how serious she was about planning the family's meals. What they called, the Sabbath meal, on Fridays was like a religious ceremony. The precious oblong gefilte fish pot, brought all the way from Eastern Europe by the master's grandmother, was taken down to bake their famous stuffed fish dish. Mrs Rodensky tried to teach her about Jewish dietary law, but she found it hard to take in all the little rules, so the mistress quickly gave up and left her be. The whole family would get excited about their meals together, and it was wonderful to see the ceremony they made of the Sabbath meal. She would set the table with a snowy-white table cloth, and all the best cutlery along with the plaited loaves which they called challah with their lovely gold crusts. The glasses would sparkle under the light from the candlesticks. She was a little awed by the devotion with which they approached the meal, as if they were going to pray, but it certainly hadn't stopped them enjoying their food.

She settled into a contented rhythm of life over the next few years. In spite of the hard, repetitive work she was glad of the measure of freedom and independence it afforded her and contrasted it with what life would have been like at home. Pleasant and plump, Willa, with her open cheery face made the kitchen a real welcoming place. Her grandmother had come from Swabia in Germany in the 1850s, and Willa had learnt a lot from her. It was Willa who taught her to cook the basic stews of meat and vegetables she would rely on all of her life. Eilin remembered how proud she was of her *hasedpfeffer*, a highly flavoured rabbit stew, but her great delight was her sauerkraut. They both enjoyed the harvest ritual of making up the barrels of sauerkraut that were to last the year. Willa would get her friend Hans Klieber to help her with this. She told her that his father had been an itinerant *krauthoble* r, someone whose job it was to shave the mounds of cabbage into threadlike strands, and Hans knew how to do this too. They would scrub the barrels, then salt the cabbage and pound and layer it, before covering it with a cloth weighted down by a stone. It would create its own pickling brine which would be skimmed away every week and the cloth rinsed.

She would sometimes join Willa and her family at one of the many beer gardens on the East Side where they gathered to drink beer and eat their sausage, hams and frankfurters. She was surprised at how jovial these gatherings remained, with very little drunkenness. Even their enormous *volkfests* always seemed to be orderly and well behaved. She recalled the year she was invited by Willa to one in Brooklyn's Ridgewood park, where the cook's singing club which they called, a *verein,* joined with a lot of the other *vereins* (many New York Germans were members of these clubs), and you'd be amazed at the colossal amounts of food they consumed. There were pyramids of sauerkraut, herring and potato salad, the usual hams and all kinds of sausages as well as a continual flow of beer, and no violence. It was hard to imagine her own people managing to have such a good time without any ructions, and she felt a bit ashamed.

It was the Rodensky family who urged her to attend the night classes in English language, civics and American history, run by a nearby settlement house. They told her that this was important because she would influence how their two little girls, aged nine and eleven, spoke. The children were already attached to her, and she needed, they said, to be well informed and able to speak good English. She began to get a lot more confident about reading and writing too, and the mistress lent her simple stories to read in order to help her with this.

This explained how Eilin had come to be so "well-spoken", something which all her neighbours remarked upon and which had indeed surprised me on first meeting her.

Eilin knew that they were not a very traditional Jewish family as they ate ham, shellfish and oysters, which were particularly popular. They also, like the Irish, ate a lot of potatoes and herrings but cooked them in all sorts of different ways. She loved it when the mistress's mother, Mrs Schoenberg, a stout old lady with a thin fuzzy moustache on her upper lip, came over, as she always did when a goose was killed, to supervise the rendering of fat. This was then stored in earthenware jars to be used throughout the months ahead. She and Willa loved the stories she told of her young days in the Lower Eastside when folk kept geese and chickens in the tenement basements, " just like your people used to keep pigs," she told Eilin. "The city's sanitary inspectors did away with all that; a pity," she added sadly. "Don't be ridiculous mother," the mistress said, "they were stinking, and the tenements were disease ridden." Old Mrs Schoenberg would throw up her eyes and shake her head for Eilin's benefit. One of the reasons she felt more comfortable with this family was because they weren't too proud to let you know that they too had been poor. She didn't feel that they looked down on her, even though she had to work as hard there as she'd had to anywhere else.

Mrs Schoenberg would sometimes ask her to accompany her back down to the teeming East Side, the area which had been the old lady's first home in New York. She seemed to relish the hubbub, though Eilin sometimes found the swirl of strange tongues, alongside the crush of shoppers, pushcart peddlers and hawkers, overwhelming. They said that it was the most crowded place on earth, and she could well believe it. With her basket over her arm, Mrs Schoenberg would push her way through the crowds, and you could see that she just loved being in the thick of it all. She'd bargain away with the pushcart vendors for foods which Eilin knew she didn't need. The markets reminded her of the *shtetlach* back home with its outdoor food-markets, Mrs Schoenberg would explain. It was strange the way she always avoided Allen Street as she tunnelled her way round Hestor and Grand Streets, but Eilin learnt later that this street was famous for its prostitutes. They both liked to watch the children playing in Seaward Park, which had been created specially for them and was supervised, but it was odd that there seemed to be even more children still playing in the streets; they must have preferred the freedom.

Sometimes they called into the imposing offices of the *Daily Forward,* a socialist newspaper which fought for worker's rights, where Mrs Schoenberg's brother Reuben worked. Mr Rodensky, her son-in-law, didn't approve of it; said it was un-American. "I don't know why," Mrs Schoenberg shrugged, "Reuben just wants everyone to have what Americans want: Och, men are strange Eilin, don't bother with them. "

They would always call into Jarmalowski's bank, where she would check her account and take out some money, and this was surely very grand. Mrs Schoenberg told her that it had been founded for poor immigrant Jews and Eilin could see that she was very at home there. She would then take her to Ratners, or another of the East Side's dairy restaurants and treat her to a plate of chopped herring and a basket of onion rolls. She loved these trips and knew, without anything ever being said, that no mention was to be made of them to the mistress. Mrs Rodensky had been educated to occupy a place in society well removed from the family's humble beginnings. Indeed, Mrs Schoenberg was very proud of her daughter and would not have approved of her making an excursion of that kind.

Sometimes as a special treat, she would be asked to take the girls to the Houston Hippodrome in East Houston Street, a Yiddish vaudeville house that showed moving pictures. The girls would beg to be taken to the local *knish* parlour afterwards where they sold only *knishes*, a rolled pastry either with cheese or meat; it was a sort of Russian peasant food, she'd heard, and it was certainly delicious. She knew that when Mr and Mrs Rodensky themselves went out into the Lower East Side, it was to one of the better class Russian, Romanian or Hungarian restaurants. There were a lot of them at that time catering to well-off folk whose parents had maybe came from those countries

She had the usual jobs to do within the Rodensky household, lighting fires, serving meals, but what she liked best was looking after Rosy, who was nine, and eleven-year-old Rebecca. She enjoyed getting them ready for school or bed, and it warmed her heart the way they trusted her with their childish confidences. Bianca, a dark wiry Sicilian woman, came to do the heavy kitchen work, and they became friends. They would take trips together down to the Sicilian candy stores in Elizabeth Street where Bianca would buy some *torrone* (a sort of nougat type sweet) for the children. At Easter time, there would be marzipan lambs and Eilin was a bit shocked to see candy statues of the Blessed Virgin or the Saints, but Bianca just laughed. It was in the Italian pushcart market in Mulberry Street that she caught her first sight of a snail peddler. He was advertising his wares on an upright board with snails clinging to it, and she vowed that she would never eat Italian food. She recalled the window box in Bianca's tiny apartment where she grew oregano, basil, mint, lettuce and tomatoes and discovered that it was the Italians who brought the tenement garden to New York immigrant life. It was Bianca also who introduced her to spaghetti and other pasta dishes.

Eilin told me that she missed this food, and I hadn't liked to point out that it was readily available and would be easy to cook even with her limited facilities.

She had her worst New York winter shortly after she went to work for the Rodenskys in December 1917. It had been quite warm for mid-December when the rain suddenly turned to snow, and the temperature plummeted to below freezing. She was sent out to the yard by Willa to bring in some wood for the stove and was knocked to her knees by a ferocious gust of icy wind. All along the street shutters were slamming, and small trees were bent over. There was a thin emaciated man struggling through the wind and snow. She felt a surge of pity for the many vagrants: you'd see them huddling in the doorways and alleys of the Lower East Side, or sleeping on park benches, shunned by passers-by as they begged for food or a few cents. Sometimes you'd see them on the waterfront staring at the ships coming into harbour, their faces full of futile longing. How could they survive this cruel weather?

She and Willa stared in astonishment at the fearful pelt-
ing snow, wondering where such a blizzard could have
come from so quickly. It went on all night and the
whole of the next day, and the city was entirely swal-
lowed up in a great whiteout. They heard later that the
winds were gusting at a ferocious speed and had driven
the snow into drifts way above people's heads, The
next day, about fifty bodies were discovered, of people
who had been caught out in the blizzard and frozen to
death. None of the shops were open, and there was
hardly a soul to be seen out in the streets. She was surprised when Peig told her later that O'Meara's Tavern
had stayed open, and that the brewer's wagon, loaded
with kegs of ale and pulled by ten massive horses, even
managed to make a delivery.

The feeling of freedom when she woke up on her day
off was always magical. If it was fine, she'd set off early
in the morning, calling into Ebinger's bakery for two of
their bagels with cream cheese for herself and Peig, for
a picnic by the river. They'd often meet in Mom's diner
near where Peig worked. She remembered the clanging
cowbells of Jacky Smalldone's junk wagon and his clar-
ion cal, "Roll up, roll up, good money for your junk,"
which made her laugh. He was a fat, bad tempered little
man who would swear at the local children, but sure
they mocked him mercilessly. He was part of the street
life, along with Micky Magner the ice man. Micky was
as good humoured as Jacky was bitter but they seemed
good friends for all that. The children would also fol-
low Micky on hot summer days, and he would let them
have slivers and shavings of ice to cool themselves
down.

She would sometimes visit Maisie, or Nora, who had
moved away from the Lower East Side to the Highbridge area of the Bronx. Eilin thought her one-bed-

roomed apartment, all to herself, the height of luxury. Nora was president of the ladies committee of the Sacred Heart parish, and was, she said herself, very efficient. They were responsible for organising fundraising activities such as dances, picnics, or sporting events. It was no wonder that it became so prosperous they were able to replace the old wooden chapel with a very handsome building in Dorset marble. A big Irish community lived there because it was near the city's transit system where so many of them worked. She would never forget the evening on which, after one of these parish events, Nora took them to the Prospect Theatre on 9th Street., to see Charlie Chaplin in *The Kid.* Oh, how they had laughed and cried - even Nora. Eilin would love to see that film again.

Looking at the childlike delight in the begrimed old face, I thought of how great it would be to bring her to see it again. I grinned then at the sudden unbidden thought that I'd also like to bring Fr Duggan to see it. He was a rather odd priest, with a certain childlike, straightforward quality to him which I found endearing. Prior to the meeting about the meals-on-wheels service in his parish the previous evening, he'd opened the door to my knock, dusting specks of sawdust from his black clerical vest and shaking hands with brisk shyness. He rarely wore his jacket in the house where he was usually involved in some woodwork project. His workmanship was quite crude but seemed to totally absorb him. This was how I would always find him whenever I called. He used the length of his arm now to wipe half the table clean of wood shavings and implements, and I was touched to see a wooden tray with cups and saucers and thinly cut slices of buttered brown bread all laid out ready to eat. "I'll just wet the tea," he said bustling about, and together we relished the simple meal. Over the months I knew him, he would make me a stool, a lovely polished blackthorn stick and frames for my two Van

Gogh prints. I loved those frames, so obviously home-made. He was always delighted to see me and would insist on making tea and serve it with the thinly cut brown soda bread, which he seemed to live on. He didn't have a housekeeper, didn't need one, he said.

CHAPTER 13

Dashed Hopes

I relished Fr. Duggan's informed interest in nature, specifically botany and geology. He it was who first introduced me to the corrie lakes of the Kerry Mountains and to the strange limestone landscape of the Burren. I marvelled at its bewildering array of flowering plants, some of which belonged to Arctic and some to Mediterranean climes. The delight of trekking that landscape was a revelation and was gratefully brought to mind decades later, on reading Moya Cannon's poem *Thirst in the Burren*

> *No ground or floor*
> *Is as kind to the human step*
> *As the rain-cut flags*
> *Of these white hills*
>
> *Porous as skin*
> *Limestone resounds sea-deep, time-deep…*

During all the time I knew Fr Duggan I never heard him utter a single religious thought or belief, and I always wondered why he'd become a priest. I asked him once when we were strolling around the foot-friendly limestone flags, and he seemed uncomfortable, saying rather vaguely, "Well you know, it seemed a good sort of thing to do, now come here and look at this little orchid," and I knew that the subject was closed.

I recalled wryly his lack of tact, which had my friends Tony and Karen vituperating against him because he refused to include their two children in first holy communion celebrations. They had wanted their children to be part of this big occasion, but Fr Duggan told the children that they could not participate because their parents didn't believe. I felt protective of the social ineptitude which characterised the old priest. I knew that diplomacy was foreign to his nature and that his black and white approach to such issues reflected his discomfort in dealing with any doctrinal or emotional complexity. Understandably Tony and Karen found it hard to share my feelings on that occasion.

The Rodenskys had a holiday camp in the Adirondack Mountains where they went every summer, and some of Eilin's best times were spent there during the early 1920s. There were a lot of cabins in the camp, and a large main house with a lounge, dining room and kitchen. Grand Central Station, where they took the train from, dazzled her with its splendour; she had never seen the like of it and could scarcely believe it was just a station. It was surely like a cathedral, grand and serene, with all sorts of arches and columns, and beautiful statues. She looked up in wonder at a ceiling which was like a starry night sky. They stopped at the Saranac Inn for breakfast before being taken by launch up the lake to the camp. Saranac Lake always seemed so still and purely blue, with the lovely cool green of the fir and spruce trees surrounding it. She shared a cabin with Frieda, Willa's cousin, hired by the family for the summer. It was a time when the family were very relaxed, and the servants too got to have lots of fun. There was a boat just for the use of the help, and they'd take it out on the lake in the evenings; she remembered singing by moonlight or visiting the servants in other camps and playing cards.

It was great, getting to meet up at beaches or parks for picnics and swimming with other family maids and their children. By then she was firm friends with Rosy and Rebecca and was surprised to hear from some of her new friends that they didn't like the children they cared for. She secretly sympathised with Rebecca's rebellious spirit when she didn't want to do her schoolwork or practise her violin, and it was easy to distract her with stories or with planning treats to come. Rosy had a special niche in her heart. She was a shy, gentle child who loved to be told stories and to tell her own, and this was a great delight to Eilin. Rosy did not like shouting, and her little hand would slip nervously into hers if Rebecca and her mother got into an argument, as they often did at that time. It was that little hand pumping nervously in hers that awoke such a fierce protective feeling in her.

That time, during the early years of the 1920s, she loved to walk around fashionable Manhattan with its sparkling stores and mansions. You could gaze forever at the glittering jewellery in Tiffany's windows and, when dressed in her best finery, she'd wander around Macy's wonderful department store. The Rodenskys lived on the less fashionable West Side, which was quieter and where prices were lower, though it had some big mansions too. She wondered what it would be like to live in one of the grand mansions around fifth and Madison avenues looking out over Central Park. She'd heard that some of them were copied from French chateaux and European Renaissance palaces. It must be great to travel to those places, surely a far cry from West Clare. It was pure pleasure to watch the elegantly dressed men and women descending from their smart cabs and motorcars outside the Waldorf-Astoria Hotel, but it was St Patrick's Cathedral, with its soaring twin spires, which touched her with personal pride. This was built by, and for, the hordes of her fellow countrymen who had swept over the great city the previous century, and indeed all the Irish were proud of it. Here in its grand interior, she felt that she too belonged in New York. She liked to sit for a while in the stillness, especially at dusk, when only the flickering candles and gaslight warmed the comforting shadows. It was surely a wonder that the rough men she knew could build something so fine.

"Well Maisie," she greeted her old cousin, frailer now, at the entrance where they met on the last Sunday of every month. There, outside the huge oak doors after Mass, the bells continued to peal their call to the faithful. Walking through Central Park at their ease, they could imagine the swamps and hills that had been drained and levelled to create this lovely place, with its landscaped lawns and ponds, woods and avenues. St Patrick's Day was another source of pride: she would make her way down to Maisie's in good time to watch the huge parade of their fellow countrymen. Jack and Jo would march with the Claremen's association and Nancy's Matty with his firemen colleagues, but there was always a good scattering of Americans there too. All the local politicians would be decked out in the green and shamrock to secure the Irish votes, and you'd know that old Ireland had left its mark on New York.

Paidi and Annie would never believe the things she'd seen. For the Lords sake, she didn't know what it was, the first time she saw a telephone. It was when she was working for the Rodenskys, cleaning out the grate in the sitting room, that the contraption on a side table started ringing very loudly. She stared, puzzled, as the mistress rushed to pick it up and started talking into it. She wondered if she was going a little mad. The mistress, when she caught her staring open-mouthed, sat down and began to laugh until there were tears streaming down her face. She was sure then that there was something seriously wrong, and she muttered, "Be at your ease Mam, I'll get you a glass of water." She ran to the kitchen where Willa was cooking and explained that the mistress had taken a turn. By the time she got back Mrs Rodensky was herself again and explained to her that it was a telephone and that on it, you could speak to people far away, even in Boston. She found it hard to believe at first.

Then there were the new motorised vehicles with taxi meters replacing the cabs and a lot of the rich people in Manhattan were buying motor cars. She remembered her first sight of one, which, she later learnt, was called an Oldsmobile, and on the very same day she saw a Cadillac. She couldn't help wondering if they were magic; to see them moving along with nothing pushing or pulling them. She was cuter by then and didn't let on that she was that surprised, it just made people laugh at you. It was outside the Vanderbilt mansion that she got her first glimpse of a Rolls Royce, all painted silver with silver-plated fittings and green leather seats, and there was a man in a matching green and silver uniform, standing proudly to attention beside it.

Paddy and she continued to meet regularly at dances and social outings. One day they went for a walk in one of New York's parks, though she didn't remember which. They paused by a lake to watch the awkward gait of a moorhen making its way towards its fellows in the shallows. There was a tiny little island just off shore. It was really one huge rock, but an elegant pine tree seemed to grow right out of the middle of it and a heron, with his pale outer plumage like a ragged cloak, stood very still underneath it. It was a scene like one of the Japanese prints in the mistress's drawing room. She was worried about the newly hatched little ducklings swimming nearby because she had once seen a heron snatching one and repeatedly ducking it under water to drown it. Paddy talked of his plans to return to Kilrush when he had a bit of money saved. He hoped to build up the family business and turning to her had said that she must have a good bit of money put by too, adding that between them they'd stir the old place up. She thought this meant that he saw them as having a future together, and she was happy. Nothing more was said when they met up, as they did every week or so at some gathering or other. She knew that he was working closely with Big Tim Sullivan at that time when prohibition was affecting the business of so many of the bars and saloons run by Irishmen. She thought that he was probably involved in bootlegging liquor illegally, but this didn't bother her as, like most of the Irish, she didn't approve of prohibition. It became more difficult for him to join them on outings or at dances, but she wasn't a bit worried, knowing him to be busy.

It was a Sunday in June 1923 – she would always remember the day – when she caught sight of them. She and her friend Mary Corrigan were wandering along Skillman Ave in Long Island on their way to her parish picnic. A young couple were watching a group of boys playing baseball not far from the railroad track. They were standing close together and smiling. It was Paddy and Peig, and she knew immediately that things were different. Mary, who also recognised them called out and they turned. She could see the shock on both their faces. They were quick to explain that they'd unexpectedly managed to get the day off, but you could see they were that uneasy it was almost laughable. Oh, she hadn't felt like laughing, she felt numb, and humiliated too, because Peig knew of her hopes about Paddy.

Nothing was ever said, but after that Paddy avoided her. He tried his old bantering ways sometimes when they did run into each other, but she would just ignore him or stay blankly silent, and he quickly gave over. It was Peig's treachery that hurt her most. Their friendship had been her greatest comfort over all the years since she arrived in New York, and she now felt that it must have been a hollow thing, and she was very lonely. Peig tried to see her many times, but she wouldn't see her; she'd say she was too busy, and so Peig stopped coming round.

It was about two years later that she heard they were married, and that Paddy, with the help of Big Tim, had opened his own dance hall in the Chelsea area. There was no more talk of returning to Kilrush, and she never knew why Peig hadn't married Mick O'Meara as she'd hinted she would. Maybe he didn't come up to scratch, or she decided that Paddy was a better bet. At any rate, she knew that it was the pain of this, alongside the fact that Rebecca and Rosy, now seventeen and nineteen, were moving out of her life, (in fact Rebecca had already gone to college and Rosy was planning to go the following year) that led to the decision which would bring her back to West Clare.

I felt pretty dismal myself as I drove home that evening through the restless grey desolation of a rain-whipped landscape. The wind-blasted trees were twisted and deformed by frequent gales. It was no consolation to recall sunnier days when I'd found them charming and characterful. I reflected on the crossroads facing me as I pondered my own future. I loved my work but was undeniably lonely, and the thought of facing into another winter in the isolation of my flat above an empty shop felt very bleak at times. My American friend was keen for us to pursue our relationship and to test this out by setting up home in Dublin together; it did seem tempting.

CHAPTER 14

New York Watches the Fight for Independence

I was increasingly uneasy about the weight of expectation attached to my professional role. There were a number of referrals, sometimes from local priests, which clearly related to situations where sexual abuse was taking place within families. I assumed that knowledge of this had come through the confessional and that the priests were able to persuade the perpetrators to accept a referral for help. This must have been a relief for the priest but for me, it was a terrifying minefield. I was only recently qualified, and my knowledge of the issues around this complex and emotionally charged area was rudimentary. I would later cringe to remember some of the half-baked theories that had informed my approach, such as the possibility of collusion by the mother because of her own distaste for the sexual side of the marital relationship. Thankfully time would draw a veil over what, if anything, I did or said, but I remembered my own father's stunned disbelief when I told him of the reality of such abuse of children. This old-fashioned and very decent Tipperary farmer stared at me in disbelief. "Ah, no Judy" (for some unknown reason he always called me Judy), he said, "that could never happen", and when I insisted that it was so, he became very agitated, and spitting slightly, as he was wont to do when distressed, asserted that, they must be Protestants so. It was very hard

114

for him to accept my assurances that I was dealing with Irish Catholics.

Eilin had always written to her sister Bride and her mother, usually including a few dollars each month, but it was her correspondence with her cousin Annie married to a farmer in Doonbeg, that kept her up-to-date both with family and general events in Ireland. The years leading up to the First World War, the events of 1916 and the Irish Free State had been very exciting for the Irish in New York. All around her, from the priests at Mass and friends involved in politics, she heard of strong opposition to the US entry into the war. Then, there was a lot of confusion when John Redmond, the leader of the Irish Home Rule party, called upon the Irish to support the war effort. He believed that Ireland would be rewarded with home rule when it was over, and some people thought this made sense.

Lots of the Irish thought the 1916 rising a foolhardy venture, but it was music to her ears and those of her friends. It was surely glorious to hear about the girls fighting side by side with the lads when there was a warship firing on Dublin. Afterwards, when they executed all the leaders, oh, there was great anger against England then, and a lot of support for Sinn Fein and the war of independence that followed. Over the next few years, the stories were all about how the war for independence was going, which side had given in, and if any of the volunteers were laid low. The English were full of anger and rage because of the damage caused by the volunteers. Sure there was wholesale plundering afoot, and many's the RIC barracks that were set on fire. The English were mad, too, because of how true the Irish were to each other as they had thought them a people of no heed. They wondered how they came by the arms, but the Irish had a lot of friends, especially in America.

Annie had been to Limerick at that time and wrote about the crowds milling around amid the horses, carts and drays, and the motor cars, some of which were carrying British officers. The stirring sound of martial music and the drab khaki of soldiers were everywhere, and she caught sight of a Crossley army lorry as the military band marched towards them. She asked the tram driver why there were so many soldiers, and he explained that they were recruiting volunteers to fight for Belgium. Why weren't they fighting for Ireland, Annie asked, and he pointed to a handful of men dressed in green uniforms, "that lot over there are." She heard one of them call out, "Why die for an Empire that oppresses you?" "It's to stop them Germans murdering all the Belgian babies," the driver said to Annie. She stared at him, shocked, but he just grinned sardonically. She saw the police moving the volunteers on, and clearing a space beside a platform which had a big banner on it proclaiming, "God Save Belgium and Ireland from the Huns." A lot of the young men in and around Kilrush joined the British Army because of poverty and unemployment. They were probably bored too and thought they were in for a great adventure. However, it was the men in the green uniforms who were to strike the blow for Ireland's freedom, and like most of the Irish in New York, she identified herself with this fight.

Annie's account of "the rough ugly lot" – the Black and Tans – they sent over from England at that time shocked her. They were often drunk and would take pot shots at anything that moved, whether animal or human. They came into Annie's own home one day when they were searching every house and cabin in the county. Her mother-in-law took down the picture of the 1916 leaders, which was hanging on the wall beside that of the Sacred Heart before they arrived. They were all trembling when the soldiers filled the little house, and Eilin sensed her relief when she wrote: "that by the grace of God they went their way without doing us any harm." Two local boys, Willie Shanahan and Mikie McNamara, blamed for the death of the director of the British secret service in the area, were tortured and killed, and Annie wrote of how she cried for the care-free little boys she remembered. They were buried in Doonbeg cemetery on Christmas day,

Her account of the shooting of Gerry Murphy, the son of a neighbour and a volunteer, incensed Eilin. He was shot in the back when trying to get away over the fields. Not long after that, when Annie was out walking with her cousin Maggie, they heard the lorries coming down the boreen towards them, and jumped over the wall, lying down behind it. A bunch of black and white cows stopped their munching to stare at them which made her want to laugh, but she knew it was hysteria because her heart was in her mouth. It was a good while before the terror that was on everyone at that time passed.

They all wanted the volunteers to win and were glad to give them food and shelter when they asked. There were nights when Annie had to leave her nice warm bed when a knock on the door at midnight meant that some tired young man needed it for the rest of the night. They'd always pass on any useful information about the movements of the Tans or the RIC in the area and knew that this was essential for their own intelligence people. They were all proud of the fact that they were able to do their bit to protect the brave lads taking on the might of the British Empire, and they but poorly armed. "But to tell you the truth," Annie wrote, "we were frightened of them too at times. Anybody who informed on them would be shot," and she described the awful case of a young boy of fifteen, from above in Ennis, who had joined the volunteers, but when caught and beaten by the Black and Tans had given them information. He was executed by his fellow volunteers, and she thought that very hard, sure he was only a child. They were hard men, but she supposed they had to be. They were always a bit uneasy when the volunteers were around because that meant that the Tans would not be far behind, and they were truly terrified of them.

Annie wrote a vivid account of the evening when she went out to tie up the cow and found five big men sitting around on the hay. Their guns were glinting in the fitful light cast by the storm lantern which they placed on one of the roof-beams, and they were cramming their cartridges with buckshot. She knew that some of them had been soldiers in the Great War and that many had been on the run for a year or more, hiding out in sheep shelters, abandoned houses or barns. They all looked tough, and she thought that they'd probably become hardened to their existence. She described a dog barking, and the sky full of stars. She was surprised that it all seemed so strangely peaceful. They left very early the next morning, and she shivered as she watched them leaving through the white mist; giants looming out of the fog.

It was a few years before the peace came, and they had Michael Collins, God be good to his soul, to thank for that. It was terrible to think that after achieving a treaty and independence, Irishmen would start killing each other over some oath of allegiance, and trying to keep that crowd in the North with us. She thought the souls of the blackguards who shot Michael Collins would never rest easy. It was with disbelief that she gazed at the pictures of his fine young body laid out in state and covered by the Free State flag; he who had led the Irish to freedom. She could never take to De Valera after that, and had no time for his reputation as a daily Mass goer and communicant. If he was that holy, he should have stopped all the killing. Oh, they'd surely been bitter times. She knew that there was a lot of support for De Valera in New York, and many was the heated argument that spilled over into an ugly fight. It was a terrible thing to hear of Irishmen killing each other, and even brothers who had been friends from childhood now full of hatred. Annie wrote of a relative up by Quilty, who had died of a broken heart when one of her sons was shot, and the other refused to come to his funeral.

It was around this time that Eilin's parents died within nine months of each other, and it was a very low period for her. Her father was struck down by a heart attack, but she never knew the cause of her mother's death. She sickened and died within four weeks so it was probably cancer. There was no question of going home, though by then she had saved enough money to pay her fare. In any case by the time the letters with the news of the deaths arrived, the funeral and burials were well over. She felt herself to be cut adrift from everyone then. She would spend hours sitting in the soft candle-light of the church, where she would pray for her parents and talk to them. The air carried a trace of incense and the scent of candles, and she watched the shifting patterns as the light from the windows slashed across the benches and floor. In the stillness and silence, she found some ease from the harsh loneliness.

I had been given a tape of Otis Reading singing ….(Sittin'On) The Dock Of The Bay, and the lyrics would always recall to mind the loneliness of Eilin's experience then.

> *I left my home in Georgia*
> *Headed for the Frisco Bay*
> *'Cause I had nothin' to live for*
> *It look like nothin's gonna come my way...*

CHAPTER 15

The Return and the Wedding

It was Monday, and I was still tingling from my walk in the Burren the previous day. The sun had been unseasonably warm for mid-April, and the little road I had wandered along was hedged by the delicate green flush of the hawthorn mingling with the starry white of blackthorn blossom. Flocks of fieldfares wheeled ahead of me as I disturbed their resting places in passing, and a wash of bird song from robins, warblers, wagtails and blackbirds floated over my day. The clean grey stretches of limestone, silvered by the sun, dazzled me and I got out the sunglasses. In the mini-ravines of the fissured escarpment, I gazed at the vibrant blue of the gentians; an identical hue to that used by Henry Clarke in his lovely stained glass windows in the church in Kilrush. Scarlet orchids and the blue-purple violets flourished there too, alongside the sturdy little holly and rose bushes. Later, as the sun was setting, I eased myself down the flaggy shore to the sea. It was a day of grace and one that would later be brought to mind by Seamas Heaney's poem *Postscript* …

> *And sometime make the time to drive out west*
> *Into County Clare, along the Flaggy Shore*
> *In September or October, when the wind*
> *And the light are working off each other*
> *So that the ocean on one side is wild*
> *With foam and glitter…*

Eilin was caught off guard by the surge of misery and loneliness that overwhelmed her that time when she decided to come home. Things had happened of course; Paddy and Peig married and, though she always had a welcome for her, Maisie was fully occupied with her growing brood of grandchildren, and sure they were her delight. It was her growing sense of loneliness within the Rodensky household that decided her. She had been lulled by their kindness, and by the little girls' need of her, into believing herself part of the family. Now they were grown up, and while they always seemed glad to see her, and would make time for a quick visit, she knew that they no longer needed her and were caught up in their own lives. It was only natural, but it was hard to feel herself of so little account. She'd come to hate it too, when all their young friends would expect her to do tasks for them, calling her familiarly and with little respect by her first name. It was as if they were entitled, that they sort of owned her. She didn't used to mind it, all the maids were called by their first name, but now that she was older, and she'd noticed that even shop assistants were given the title of Miss, she didn't like it. Surely she was due more respect.

When Willa left to get married, the mistress agreed that her job as cook be taken by her niece Frieda who would share Eilin's little bedroom. She had liked sharing her room with Willa, they were friends, and she liked Frieda, but she was just a young girl, and she didn't want to share her little bit of privacy with her. Surely as a woman of thirty-four years, with no other home, she had some entitlement to a bit of private space. She explained this to the mistress who was sympathetic, but clear that she didn't have two rooms to spare. During this conversation, Mrs Rodensky also asked if she would take on laundry and ironing duties, now that the girls no longer needed her services. She broke down and sobbed then, and the mistress was truly alarmed. It was because her lowly status as a servant was brought home to her, and she knew that it was her work, not herself that was wanted.

She missed her mother sorely at that time and was full of pain at the thought the careless letters she had dashed off to her over the years. It was then too that she remembered Hannah, who had come to work for the Rodensky family one summer in the Adirondack Mountains. Hannah was a black woman born in New York, whose grandmother was from Alabama. Mrs Rodensky had asked them to take her with them when they were visiting with the other servants, but they hadn't done so. They thought her different, being black, not one of them, and she walked funny. She didn't seem to expect anything; her face was always very still. The second time Mrs Rodensky asked them to take her, Hannah said quietly that she'd rather not go out. They left her alone all that summer, and she was only a young girl away from her family. She wept now for the loneliness of this girl, and for her own misery.

About that time, Annie was writing to her about the negotiations Dinny, the parish matchmaker, was undertaking on behalf of her neighbour Peadar O'Brien. He was a man in his mid-thirties who was said to be a very good farmer. His land was well tilled and maintained, and he had some cattle as well as sheep. He lived with his mother in a three-roomed cottage, whitewashed and clean with a well-kept cobbled yard and three neat sheds for the hens, geese, pony and sidecar. Mattie Hogan, the father of the girl he was great with, wouldn't pay the dowry they expected even though, according to Dinny, he had cartloads of money, and Peadar's mother wouldn't budge until he did. "Well," Annie had written, "in the heel of the hunt didn't the girl skedaddle off to England with Danny Loughlin from above in Ennis who hadn't a penny to his name. Mattie was very sore then, and Peadar's mother was getting worried that Peadar might do the same, and bedad it would serve her right," she finished.

It was on an impulse, after getting this letter that she wrote to Annie, wondering if a match might be made between this Peadar and herself. She told her of the dollars saved that she could bring to the farm, and described her housekeeping experience and skills. She was dazed by the speed with which things were taken out of her hands then, and the next year passed in a deluge of correspondence which finalised the negotiations and arrangements for her return. Her sessions with the dressmaker added to her sense of exhilaration. Together they pored over patterns before settling on two tailored costumes, one with a straight skirt and the other with little kick pleats which she thought she would wear for the wedding. In addition, she bought sheets, pillow slips, towels and a tablecloth as well as a beautiful Tara brooch in silver and Connemara marble for old Mrs O'Brien. She sensed from Annie's letters that Peadar's mother was more enthusiastic about the match than Peadar, and she felt a twinge of pity for the young man who'd lost the girl he wanted.

Surprisingly she didn't worry on her own account. Even if she didn't much like her mother-in-law, she'd have her own home, and besides, the old woman wouldn't live forever and then she'd be mistress. She only offered half the sum of her savings as dowry, the other half she'd keep safe for herself in case she ever needed it. In New York, she'd seen too many miserable women and children living with men who would treat them very badly, often violent and drunk; the drink was surely a great curse on the Irish. You'd not often see Italians or Germans being so drunk and violent. It was terrible to see so many destitute women, trying to raise a family of young children single-handedly in poverty and hunger, while the father either drank his earnings or deserted the family. She'd protect her nest egg of savings, and if she was unhappy, sure, she'd be able to come back to New York. She knew now that she'd always be able to earn her living, and that helped to make you feel a bit more secure.

She had little memory of the voyage home, but as Ireland drew near feelings of anxiety began to crowd in; what sort of a future had she signed up for? Once she stayed out on deck the entire night watching a pale crescent moon and wondering if she'd done the right thing; well, she could hardly back out now. She listened to the herring gulls and the guillemots screeching as they whirled and swooped in the wake of the big ship easing itself into the curve of the harbour. A wave gently doused the porthole window of her cabin and dribbled soothingly down the glass. Up on deck, the clamour of the gulls filled the air, and she noticed two cormorants standing sentry on rocks out from the shore. The clouds, which had been surging across the sky, opened to reveal the glowing colours of a perfect rainbow. This was surely a good omen, and there was her sister Bride on the shore waving to her. She had come back from London and taken the train to Queenstown, now called Cobh, to meet her. She cried with relief then, and Bride patted her shoulder much as Maisie had done some seventeen years before when she arrived in New York. The sisters looked at each other, struggling to recognise in the smart young women they'd become the barefooted children they'd once been. Both wore tailored suits and little close-fitting cloche hats, and Eilin was glad that what she'd worried

125

might be a too daringly shortened skirt was matched by Bride's.

It was sad to see the port she remembered as an elegant place of dignified buildings and flowered civic gardens now looking very bedraggled and lifeless. A lot of the road signs were in Gaelic, and they seemed somehow foreign and unexpected. She sighed as they settled into the train for the final stages of her journey home. The window latch was loose in their carriage and rattled all the way back to Limerick. She stared at the burnt out relics of fine old houses, whose crumbling estate walls no longer kept anyone out. Up a river valley lined with dark trees she caught a glimpse of what must have been a beautiful home. Its walls were a pale rain-washed yellow in colour, and the paint was peeling off the wide handsome door. The empty elegant windows looked out on the lonely neglected lawns while rooks flew over the chimneys of the roofless house. They passed through towns whose ruined buildings and mud covered streets they glimpsed from station platforms. Bride told her of the great damage done by the civil war and thanked God that this was now in the past. Indeed, she was to discover that the tensions and rifts remained very near the surface, and would break out with frightening frequency during the first decade of her return home. She noticed, too, how careful people were to avoid any talk that might stir up angry feelings born of the civil war hostilities.

There was a meeting with the matchmaker and her brother, and the arrangements for the wedding were finalised. It was fine and warm a few days later when they drove over to meet Peadar and his mother, and little puffs of dust rose from the horse's hoofs as they trotted into the clean cobbled yard. The sun shone on the white walls and the golden thatch of the little house, and she thought it beautiful. Peadar was a tall angular man of about thirty-eight years, his face weather beaten and thin, with little crow's feet of humour around his eyes. She could see that he wasn't easy in his dark blue serge suit which was clearly on its first outing, and taking off his cap shook hands shyly with her. She was touched by the expression of kindness and hopefulness with which he regarded her and she smiled back warmly. Mrs O'Brien seemed frail and bent, older that her seventy-one years. She was busy and wiry in her movements, and her hair was completely white. It was surely a good thing that she and her son were so nervous because it put Eilin at her ease. She complimented them on their lovely home and on the great tea with apple pie and homemade fruit cake. She was able to tell them about one or two people she'd known who came from their parish, and soon Mrs O'Brien was asking her all sorts of questions about New York.

Peadar was quiet when they went alone for a walk after tea. Aware of his bashfulness, she told him that she knew she was a stranger to him but that she would do her best to make him a good wife. She talked about her life in New York in service, and he described his farm and goods and stock. Sure little did he know, poor man, that she was just longing for a home to call her own where she'd belong, and she wasn't worried about cattle or fields. She went back to Kilbaha with a lighter heart the following day to spend a few weeks with her own people before the wedding. It was a peaceful time reclaiming the landscape of her childhood. She breathed in the reek of turf smoke all round her; it was the smell of home. She'd forgotten how remarkable were the shapes forged out of the rocky coastline by the Atlantic, and gazed at the ocean coursing and ebbing in and around the wonderful natural arches of the Bridges of Ross, its might temporarily contained. The quiet lanes between the flattish fields and bogs were restful too, and the monbretia, thyme and saxifrage growing wild there seemed like old friends out to welcome her. It was good to become easy again with her brothers and Bride, who had all seemed like strangers at first.

The wedding took place in the nearby church, Star of the Sea, where she'd gone to Mass with her family and the neighbours as a child, and where she made her first holy communion. She cried to see the little wagon known as the ark now having pride of place within the church. It was around this little mobile wagon that her grandparents and their neighbours had gathered and knelt for Sunday Mass, whatever the weather, when the local land agent refused them permission to build a church. Afterwards, she and Peadar were in the first trap of the procession of horse-cars, mostly sidecars but a couple of traps too, that made its way down the little green road outside Doonbeg to the O'Brien's house. A good number of the people from the village were at the wedding and now they all piled into the house and tucked into a feast of bacon, fowl, cakes and lots of good things to eat, as well, of course, as tea, porter, whiskey and wine; oh there was surely no shortage that day. She was right merry then, as the musicians, well oiled with whiskey and porter, played away for the dancing. Peadar wouldn't dance, and she thought his mother looked a bit severe, but she didn't care, hadn't she paid for them all to have a grand time. It was a happy day for her.

The sky was leaden with cloud as I strolled along the great curving beach of Doughmore bay. I was cheered by the magical little islet of brightness where the sun pierced a sliver of light through that dense mass of cloud. I thought about the strangeness of men and women coming together in the pragmatic way that Eilin and Peadar had. The elemental sound of the black-backed gulls swirling around seemed to mock my more romantic aspirations, and my thoughts turned to the imminent arrival of Bob, my American boyfriend, for a week-long stay. I was both excited and apprehensive about this, and it was a reflection of the changing attitudes in Ireland of the Seventies that in spite of my public profile in the town, I wasn't bothered about him staying with me. His being different, of New York Jewish background, was a release from the comforting but sometimes oppressive sameness of the surrounding culture. It was hard to disentangle ephemeral factors such as this from the more substantial sources of the attraction, but this week would probably be a decisive one for my future.

CHAPTER 16

Eilin Settles Into a Changed Ireland

I was light-hearted; Bob and I had relished our week together. We delighted in a shared zest for music and books and the new worlds revealed in our separate tastes. The little Morris Minor resounded to the lyrics of Joni Mitchell, Bob Dylan and Neil Young as it rattled around the byways of West Clare. In the evening, I cooked, and he put on the music of BB King, Otis Reading or some other great blues musician. Afterwards, I introduced him to the music of Sean O'Riada or Planxty and was warmed by his appreciation while he, in turn, opened up for me the work of writers such as Saul Bellow and Knut Hamsun which I planned to read over the coming months. He was leaving the following day and was cooking a final meal that evening. The hedges along the little green road going to Eilin's house were full of pink campion, fat yellow buttercups, purple tufted vetch and lovely blue forget-me-nots. I picked and arranged these with long elegant grasses into a little posy, which I laid down carefully by the bridge to be collected on my return to the car.

It was during the weeks following the wedding that Eilin began to panic. It was so quiet; Peadar was up early and out milking the cows by the time she rose. His mother, Cait, was always up before him and had the porridge ready. It was as if she'd slipped into lives that had nothing to do with her; didn't really need her. She was used to lots of lively chat and was unnerved by the quiet monosyllabic responses of Peadar and his mother. It was disturbing the way they were happy to be silent for such long periods. They would sometimes talk of local events and the weather in Gaelic, and though she understood, it was a matter of pride to her that she only spoke in English. She knew that she spoke good English; it was her achievement, and she'd not have it taken from her. She found the stillness of the fields and the boreens strange, and even the smell of the wet turf and rain felt foreign. There were so many grey wet days, how could she ever have longed for this seeping wet dismal country? The one relief was the ease with which she and Peadar turned to each other in bed. While this too was a silent process, she knew that she gave him pleasure and found some comfort in it. She would sometimes catch him glancing softly at her with a sense of wonder. Nevertheless, she didn't feel she belonged in that silent little house down the lonely boreen, where only men on their way to the bog passed by from one day to the next.

"Dia dhuit Eilín ..." Annie, whose soft dimpled arms were covered in flour, greeted her, continuing to knead the dough on the floured surface of the table. She was a large, squarely built woman, whose placid good humour and common sense had tided Eilín over the loneliness of those first years in Doonbeg. She wandered across the couple of fields that separated their homes most days and was soothed by her welcome. Annie's admiring comments on her newly bought finery softened her suggestion that this should be kept for special occasions, and that to dress plainly would be more acceptable at least in the beginning. It takes time, and you need to be patient, she'd say while helping her with some of the skills she needed in her new life. She it was who taught her how to milk, and then to separate the

cream out and churn it into butter. This was put into firkins to be sold at the weekly butter markets in Kilrush. Like her neighbours, she got to enjoy the buttermilk remaining and found it a refreshing drink and great for making soda bread, which Annie had shown her how to bake in the pot oven. Together they'd knead the dough and dampen it with spring water and fresh milk while she told Annie stories about her life in New York. It was a revelation to see how wonderfully the bread baked in this flat-bottomed pan with a tightly fitting lid. You'd place it on the fire with glowing embers on top, to create an even heat throughout. Fowl and meat of any kind would be cooked in the same way and always tasted delicious. She'd also shown her how to bake griddle bread on the round iron plate which stood on a little trivet over the turf.

There continued to be a lot of unrest at that time and, like her neighbours, she was wary of expressing any political views. She knew that passions ran high on both sides of the lingering civil war divide, but was shocked the day Peadar returned from Kilrush with news of the death of a local detective. He had received a box with a note signed, "from a farmer". It had contained a bomb which exploded killing the poor man and wounding his colleagues. It was a good number of years after the end of the civil war in 1931 when Willie McInerney was shot and wounded on his own doorstep inside in Kilrush. A note was pinned to the door saying "spies beware". Peadar told her that Dev and Fianna Fail had a lot of support in Clare and advised her not to be saying too much against him. She heard he'd been heckled at a meeting in Kilrush not long after she returned, but it became clear as the years went on that his support was very substantial. Dozens of bonfires blazed from the hillsides and crossroads of Clare the night he won the election in February 1933. Even though she didn't like him, she and Peadar went to see the victory celebrations. It had surely been something to see that torchlight procession and the two score horsemen accompanying him to the platform in Kilrush.

During her childhood, she remembered, people had been peaceful in spite of the awful times they'd been through. The Ireland she arrived back to was different. Folk were only too ready to take action if they didn't like the decisions that were made. There were ructions shortly after her return when the schoolmaster Mr Lennon retired, and Fr Vaughan took possession of the schoolhouse and installed that teacher from Limerick. Sure the poor man was beaten out of the place with sticks, stones and bottles because the local people wanted Mr Lennon's son. Then there was the time they'd fired shots into Patrick Clery's house in Knock because he gave lodgings to the new postman, and they didn't want him, they wanted a local man. She thought that maybe it was that they'd got used to violence over all those years of fighting, but it wasn't a good thing.

On top of that, there were endless strikes by the dockers, and sometimes the mill workers in at Glynn's flour mills and even in the creamery once. These too were marked by violence. A lot of the trouble was between members of the Irish Transport & General Workers Union and non-union members. Back in May 1932, there was a bomb thrown through the bar window of Williams hotel in Frances Street. This was owned by Ryans & Sons, with whom the dockers were in dispute, and the following winter their goods store was bombed. She was in Kilrush when another dispute broke out, and revolver shots were fired as a bomb exploded in Cappa. Her mother's cousin, Bessie Maloney, was in fearful anxiety during those times. She was a

widow, poor soul, as her fisherman husband had
drowned leaving her with two young boys to raise, and
they had grown up a bit wild. They were among the
striking dockers and Bessie was torn between her terror
of them getting killed or being charged by the police
for crimes of violence, and her fear for their immortal
souls. The priests were certainly against the violence
and didn't approve of the unions. There was a lot of
talk about communism then, and Bessie told her that
the Bishop had preached about its evils when he was
down in Kilrush for the confirmations. Neither she nor
Bessie rightly knew what this meant at the time, but
were aware that the priests linked it with union activity
and Bessie, who was a very religious woman, worried.

Though most of her neighbours travelled by ass or
horse and cart, quite a few of them had bicycles, and by
the time Sonny was born in 1930 she had persuaded
Peadar to buy one. She always thought that motor cars
were fearful machines, and all the accidents that time
proved just how right she was. She knew one of the
four women injured when a car with six passengers
overturned near Kilrush shortly after her return, and a
couple of years later a motor car ran into a milk cart on
the Ennis road. When she heard the following year that
an ambulance had skidded into a big hole on the way to
hospital in Ennis, she vowed that she'd rather go to
hospital in the ass and cart.

The familiar greeting, " 'Tis a grand day Mam, bedad it
is," no matter what the weather, always told her that
Billy O'Meara and his bicycle had arrived. Red-haired
and freckled, his plump round face perspiring from his
exertions as he unclipped his trousers at the ankle, Billy
came every Saturday or Sunday there was a hurling or
football match on in any parish within travelling dis-
tance. He and Peadar had been friends since school

days, and both were mad GAA men. They were beside themselves with excitement the day Clare was playing Cork in Kilrush before a crowd of six thousand spectators in June 1929, but wasn't it a terror to say that she'd forgotten who won. She hadn't forgotten however that Kilrush beat Quilty in the senior football championships at Miltown Malbay in September 1937, with four thousand spectators looking on because that was the last match poor Peadar ever went to. He would be dead within two years. He used to say that it was the GAA that helped people forget about the hatred of the civil war years. In all those hundreds of parishes up and down the country, old resentments were forgotten in the excitement of the games, and the local rivalries held little of that bitterness. "We beat Miltown Malbay Mam"- the excitement of Sonny in 1949 when he was just nineteen brought Peadar to mind when Kilrush won back the football title after a lapse of eleven years.

"Patrick Kelly told me there'll be a set, up at Jackie Ryan's tonight." Peadar, on returning from the forge where he had the horse shoed, told her. Patrick was from Cree and a great fiddler and her heart lightened as she always loved to dance. He would sit in a corner just back from the hearth, under a shelf with a lamp that had a red globe and two wicks in it because there was no electricity that time, and he'd play away lost in the music. He was a great one for the airs, but he'd play for the sets too. Peadar would give her the odd dance but would rather stand and listen to the music or singing, and she loved it when he encouraged Billy to dance with her. Billy was a shy man, and he reddened when you talked to him, but he was a grand dancer, and she recalled the occasional night when the other dancers would ease away to leave them dancing alone, their steps getting more and more complex and the tempo wild and fast. They always got a great round of applause then. She smiled to remember one of those nights when the local lads were up to their tricks and one of them put a piece of tin through the hasp on the door from the outside so that you couldn't get out. Peadar had to go through a window to let them out, and it was a very small one. Oh, he was cursing something terrible though he was a thin man.

Peadar surely loved the music. She was worried the night he didn't return from Kilrush until well after midnight. It was a cold and wet morning when he set out, and she ran after him with a bit of old sacking to throw over his shoulders. He was taking his boots to the cobbler to be repaired and collecting a bag of oatmeal, so she expected him back by early afternoon. It wasn't like Peadar to drink too much, but that night he was very well lubricated. He had driven in on the ass and cart which was a lucky thing, because it was the ass, who by then had more wits about him than Peadar, that drove him home. He told her that he heard the famous Dublin piper Johnny Doran playing his pipes sitting on a butter box in the square in Kilrush, and after a while they all went into Crotty's public house and had great music for the rest of the day and a good part of the evening. Mrs Crotty herself being such a fine musician meant that they had many good times there of an evening. Before Sonny was born, they'd sometimes go over to Cree and spend the evening in the Kelly's house. Patrick would sit down in a corner by the open fire, and play away every tune he had and never go back over one, for he was a great man for the music.

The government brought in the Public Dance Halls Act in 1935, and this brought an end to house dances, because the local clergy and the Gardai often used it to ban them, and people could be fined if they were caught. Sure they carried on having them for a good while in West Clare, but with so many of the young ones leaving the country, and the ban, they'd faded out altogether by about 1950. She couldn't believe it was true at first, why would anyone want to put a stop to something that was such an innocent pleasure. Then she heard that John Harrison inside in Kilrush had invited Johnny Doran for a night's music, and the house was full and didn't the guards come and clear the whole place. She knew too that a William Kelly up in Longford was prosecuted when a local Garda sergeant found thirty people dancing in his kitchen and a further fifteen playing cards. After that, it was mostly in the parish halls they held dances, supervised by the parish priest. But just like in New York, it didn't take long for the commercial dance halls to spring up where people felt freer, and could enjoy the jazz music which was becoming popular. You'd hear young folk singing Bing Crosby and Frank Sinatra tunes because by then people had gramophones and radios. She was surprised that Sonny never seemed that keen to go to the dances as he got older, more like his father, she thought.

Peadar thought they should ask Patrick Kelly to give Sonny lessons in the fiddle, but much as she loved the music and dancing she didn't want Sonny to learn the fiddle. She knew how the music and dancing could lead people astray; sure she'd seen how musicians would often neglect the farm and stay out all night carousing and sometimes stay away for days at a time. There was that morning she was coming back from the beach at about six thirty, having gone down with Peadar who was going to the fishing that day. It was very fine weather that time, and she could see the dust being raised over the ditch where there was a man, and he wasn't a young man either, dancing on the road with Jacky Molloy playing the fiddle for him. Wasn't that some picture at six o'clock of a fine summer's morning, and he above only playing the fiddle and your man dancing out on the road; well that was surely how many a farm went to rack and ruin.

I had my own memories of dancing in the huge barn-like ballrooms constructed to accommodate the showband craze which swept the country, during the late Fifties and Sixties. At its height, there were four hundred and fifty ballrooms spread across the country and some of these held up to four thousand people. The plethora of musical ingredients that made up this scene included traditional and ballad influences, jazz and rock'n roll. I remembered some of the well-known names – Brendan Bowyer's Royal Show band, the Dickie Rock band. There was always a huge crush in the ladies rooms, and I could still see the row of anxious, made up faces reflected in the long mirrors. Though I hadn't thought of it as such, it can only have been sex that ensured our weekly subjection to the torture of lining up along one side of the ugly, hangar-like dancehalls, to be scrutinised like animals on show. Few of the gangling awkward youths, or worse still, older sleazy characters looking for "a bit of action", lived up to aspirations nourished on a diet of gooey romantic fiction full of dashing manly heroes.

Oh well, I sighed, thinking of my own "romantic enough" situation. I planned to drive Bob to Shannon the following morning for his flight back to London. We had discussed his proposal that we should both look for jobs in Dublin and set up home together. He was optimistic about our relationship and felt that it had a future; the logical next step was to test this out. I had agreed, aware that my slight sense of flatness was probably due to idiotic childish longings, as I thought rather crossly that there wasn't much difference between the practical arrangements being proposed by Bob, and Eilin and Peadar's pragmatic contract.

CHAPTER 17

Her Child is Born

When I was newly arrived in West Clare, the local community nurse had pointed out a little cottage where a woman, then in her eighties, lived, an almost total recluse since the age of twenty-one when she'd had an illegitimate child. Childbirth for all women was tough and hard. Maggie told me of a travelling woman known to her mother, who moved through the country living in a tent, and who had thirteen or fourteen children, all born at the side of the road without doctor or midwife. There was no transport or phones so most children were born at home, as indeed she had been, where sometimes an experienced local woman might help. I thought about the hard lives women in Ireland had endured over past decades. The all-powerful church urged them into an acceptance of their role as breeders and mothers within the confines of marriage. With no question of contraception or divorce, women struggled to cope with large families in often difficult circumstances. There was little redress from abusive situations, and any flouting of expectations met with severe censure and little or no support.

Sonny was born in 1930 when Eilin was already forty years of age, and with him was born the most powerful emotion of her life.

Exhausted and drained, she gazed at the little skinned rabbit of a son Bessie Maguire placed in her arms. She cried and whispered her thanks to Bessie, herself a mother of six, who had stayed with her throughout the eleven-hour ordeal of the birth. Bessie usually had a sharp tongue, but she was gentleness itself then, keeping up her spirits, and encouraging her to patience when she cried out in desperation. It was truly extraordinary the way you forgot the awful pain of the labour and birth so quickly, and all she felt was a fierce possessive love for her child. He would be christened Sean Peadar, but was always known as Sonny. She could hardly bear to let anyone touch him, and poor Peadar, already shy and awkward, had no chance to get close to his little son. She'd catch the odd haunting look of longing on his face as he regarded the baby, and she'd feel a bit guilty, but he was hers. Even Cait, so gentle and kind, was only allowed to care for the child when she needed to do something around the house.

Over the years, she had grown to like Cait, who was a calm peaceful woman. She was thankful for the kindly way in which she tried to ease her into her role of farmer's wife. More importantly, Cait was curious about her life in New York, and she, in turn, enjoyed her wonder at the stories of a place and life now so remote. Peadar continued to be a quiet man, who would drop into one of the pubs in the village for a pint and chat with neighbours, before returning home in the evening. After his supper, he would potter around the yard fixing implements or fences, before coming in for the rosary and bed. It was Cait who helped to assuage her need for companionship during those early years of her marriage. She had not expected to find so little social life on her return, though she enjoyed the weekly trip to the market in Kilrush to sell their butter and eggs, and there was always a bit of talk with the neighbours after Mass on Sunday, or at the shop. The men had the hurling and football matches to go to, and of course the pub, but in spite of Cait's companionship, she often felt lonely and left behind by the world.

It was on the evening of Good Friday, when Sonny was about four, that she told Cait to keep an eye on him while she milked the cows. Earlier she had gone with her on a pilgrimage to St Senan's well in Killard, which Cait liked to do on that day every year. There, with a few of the neighbouring women, they did two or three rounds of the well, saying the rosary before drinking the water. They'd looked for the fish that would mean you'd get your wish, but could see no sign of him. Coming back with the milk, she found Sonny very close to the fire and had whipped him up, shouting at Cait, who was asleep on the chair. But poor Cait wasn't asleep, she was dead. She had been sleeping off and on since her return and had just slipped away in her sleep, God forgive her, but she was more shocked by the danger to Sonny than by Cait's death, though she had been fond of the old woman and would miss her.

Later when she was laid out, they knelt to say the rosary. She glanced at Peadar's haunted face as the men hitched up the knees of their trousers and the women pulled their shawls tighter round them. The depth of his sorrow had shaken her. He sat by her coffin the whole night long as they waked her, barely greeting the friends and relatives who came to pay their respects, and taking no part in the stories and conversations about her life. Unusually that night, there was no singing or dancing; it didn't feel right in the face of Peadar's sorrow. However, the mourners were uneasy, seeing as she was an old woman who'd had a good long life. Strangely she was not jealous of the love he had for his mother. She knew, to her shame, that she exulted in his grief, seeing in it the image of the love that would tie Sonny to her.

The rain sheeted down on the black-creped hats of the men shouldering the coffin through the village the following day. The doors were closed and blinds drawn as a mark of respect. She noticed a tinker encampment on the way; just strips of canvas thrown over iron hoops to form makeshift tents. The men stood respectfully outside these, caps in hand. After Mass, the rain continued to fall, and the cawing of the crows over the bare winter trees added to the loneliness. The mourners gathered around the opened grave for the last prayers, and she felt for Peadar as he stared numbly at its side walls, pared to such a smooth finish. It was only the green of the sods, laid aside for a final cover to the grave that gave any touch of colour to the grey scene. The coffin was lowered and the first few handfuls of dirt thrown on the grass cuttings that softened the thud on the wood.

Her feeling for Peadar's loss brought them closer, and she knew that slowly but surely he was transferring his devotion to her, and she was glad of it. She was content over those next years and was only dimly aware of the changes introduced by the arrival of the wireless among the neighbours. People would gather in the houses where there was one, to listen to the news when anything important happened, like the death of Pope Pius XI, or the coronation of Pius XII. Sure they spent the entire day at the O'Briens' house the time of the Eucharistic Congress up in Dublin. There were thousands of priests and bishops from all over the world gathered up in Phoenix Park that day, and they heard John McCormack singing the *Ave Maria*. When he wasn't at a local match, Peadar was up at the O'Briens every Sunday to hear Michael O'Hehir covering the hurling or football on the wireless. All the houses with a wireless would be crammed with men listening to him, and they'd be jumping out of their breeches with excitement, the air thick with their cigarette smoke. There would be bets made and, no matter how scrambled or exciting the play, that calm voice would be as clear as daylight, telling everything happening on the pitch to thousands of listeners. The tension would be terrible, but his voice was more like that of a friend to them than a wireless commentator.

Cait's death surely left a lonely wound in her life. She knew that she had a good man in Peadar who but rarely came home drunk and was never violent , but he didn't talk to her much, and for company, he had the other men in the pub. It was the same with the neighbours, and the women took it for granted that men and women didn't spend any free time together. She was surprised to find herself sometimes thinking of the Cornish boy Josh, and how they had loved to talk and be together. She'd often look at the grey curtains of rain blotting out the dismal scrubby land while the wind-blasted down the chimney filling the room with smoke and think longingly of the vibrant streets of New York and the lively time she could be having there. But then she had Sonny, and he talked to her, the little *peata*, though it was many the fright he'd given her too. She had been very worried when, not long before his fifth birthday, there was an outbreak of diphtheria in West Clare, but thanks be to God and his Blessed Mother, he wasn't affected.

"Can I sit up front with Daddy?" Sonny's enthusiasm was contagious. He was six years old, in his first Communion shoes and short grey trousers, with the red and white pullover Annie had knitted for him. He would not let on that his shoes were uncomfortable for he knew he looked fine and was proud of it. They were setting out for Kilrush, which would be decked out in flowers and flags for the annual Corpus Christi procession, its shops and houses freshly painted or whitewashed and flying the yellow and white papal flags for the occasion. They all looked grand, Peadar in his wedding suit and new cap, and she glad that the green tweed costume she'd bought in New York still fitted her. Arriving at Bessie's, Sonny went off with some of the local children to play, while Bessie made tea. It was a couple of hours later when an anxious Peadar came back with the rumour that a child had fallen into the water off Merchant's Quay. She panicked then and set off running, pushing her way to the front of the crowd gathered around the quays. When she saw a woman rocking a little one of four or so in a shawl, she sank to the ground in relief. The child had fallen in and Patrick Walshe, a local man, had jumped in and brought her to safety. Still she wasn't easy that evening until Sonny came back, and found it hard to let him out of her sight over the next few days.

She hardly understood the gladness and contentment the child brought her. There were times when she felt weak with joy, like the day she sent him to bring in the eggs from the shed. He was only four but loved to collect the eggs from the corner behind the meal bin, where he thought the hen was trying to hide them. When he didn't return, she went out to find him. He was sitting on a patch of dirty straw, his bare feet in the muck, with a tortoiseshell kitten in his lap and a grey striped one draped over his shoulder. His little face streaked with mud beamed up at her, and she didn't know which of them was the happier. She could still see him and his great friend Charlie O'Brien setting off to fish for minnows the first day of the summer holidays when he was about seven. It was raining, but they didn't mind that, and she watched the two little bare-footed boys in their ragged trousers, with a bit of old sacking thrown over their backs for shelter, running away from her across the yard. It was as if their joy was hers. They surely taught her a lot about little boys. That first time she saw them belting each other in the yard and screaming terrible names, she had rushed out and sent Charlie home. After moping around the house for about fifteen minutes Sonny announced that he was go-ing over to Charlie's house to play, and when she pointed out that he'd said he never wanted to see him again, he just said simply, "Well I do now."

I shivered, towelling myself vigorously; the water had been freezing where I'd taken a quick dip off White Strand. I glanced at the gulls flashing black and white as they swooped over the ocean and made my way to the ruins of Doonmore castle. There I sat, looking over to Magrath Point, idly wondering who Magrath was. Down below, there were fishermen hunched against the wind and the rain, mending lobster pots. I watched a scattering of sand-pipers hugging the skirts of the incoming waves and curlews mining the mudflats for worms with their long slender beaks. A rabbit stared unblinkingly from a clump of furze bushes as I sauntered briskly over the sands. What a waste it was that Eilin, fearful of the destructive power of the sea, never brought Sonny down here, and he'd never learned to swim. It would have been such a magical envi-ronment for a child and right on her doorstep too.

CHAPTER 18

Peadar Dies and Sonny Drifts

We were in the little panelled front room of the pub in Miltown Malbay. I could see the angular raw face of the Kerryman, softened now by the poetry of his love song, the poignant *Donal Og*. His rough countryman's hand was held and tenderly pumped all the while he was singing by a tall thin man whose narrow, sensitive face jerked with a queer twitching movement, but stilled in response to the song, and was, I thought, beautiful in repose. He was accompanying and encouraging him along every note of this powerful lament of an abandoned woman. The pub went very quiet for that final verse which I had found unbearably desolate …

> *You have taken the east from me, you have taken the west from me;*
> *you have taken what is before me and what is behind me;*
> *you have taken the moon, you have taken the sun from me;*
> *and my fear is great that you have taken God from me.*

It was strange what a comfort sad music was, even more maybe than the merry tunes. It seemed to soothe away pain and loneliness, making you feel you belonged. I had been up to Miltown Malbay for the tail-end of the music festival, and on my return journey was reflecting gratefully on how I had come to know and love the rich musical heritage I felt heir to. For this, I owed a huge debt to the

Begley family of the remote Dingle peninsula whom my brother had married into. I thought of how they, and families like them scattered throughout the country, had carried that heritage with pride and confidence through the years when it was far from fashionable and indeed often looked down upon. My sister and I had been lucky enough to spend time in their home, soaking up this wealth of music during our teen years

There was a huge surge in the popularity of Irish music in the Fifties and Sixties, under the impetus of the Piper's Club in Dublin and the formation of Comhaltas Ceoltoiri Eireann. In the subsequent mushrooming of fleadhs with their vast attendances, my friends and I relished not just the music and craic, but also the bonds forged by a sense of shared identity. We were enthusiastic supporters of the urban folk revival emerging in the early Sixties and delighted in groups like the Dubliners and the Fureys, whose general demeanour and roguish ballads cocked a snook at the more conservative parochial ethos of the time. I found this liberating, reflecting as it did the social radicalism I aspired to while retaining a strong sense of Irish identity. I thought of the orchestral affirmation given to the tradition by composers like Sean O'Riada, and the international popularity of groups like the Chieftains emerging from his work, as well as the magical, innovative music of groups like Planxty.

Eilin enjoyed the bit of variety there was in farming life then. She would sometimes accompany Peadar when he set off for the creamery in Kilrush, carrying the milk churn in the flat backed cart. They bought day-old chickens there for rearing, and she loved to see Sonny's delight in the little golden feathery creatures, which they kept warm in cardboard boxes by the fire until they were ready to be put out. On an odd day, maybe when she would have eggs for sale, she'd go with

Peadar to the fair. They would harness the cart with the high slatted sides and load it up with pigs or turf but, no matter how early it was, the road was always full of friends and neighbours doing the same. There was fun along the way with lots of good humour and banter. The young men in their home-knit pullovers and peaked caps drove small bunches of cattle ahead of them with ash plants. The older men, taking a couple of calves or some bonhams to sell, would have old sacks thrown over their shoulders, to keep the rain off their well-worn suits and collarless shirts. There were hardly any women to be seen at the fair, but mostly you wouldn't want to go because there was mud and animal dung everywhere, and the sad sound of the lowing cows and calves. When it rained it was so filthy, you'd wonder if you'd ever get clean again.

The child was choking with sobs as he raced in from the yard to bury his face in her lap. "What is it child, what is it?" She was beside herself with anxiety, stroking his head, and only gradually became aware of the agonised squeals of the pig they were slaughtering out in the shed. She was used to the terrible din and indeed had hardly noticed it, but poor Sonny was tormented by the strangulated sound of the animal's agony that first time. Like all of them he got used to it and in time got to love all the coming and going of neighbours when the pig was killed and the black pudding made. They'd wash and clean the intestines a couple of times, and then after they'd stirred in the oatmeal, onions and spices, fill them with the blood taken from the pig. You'd have to boil them then, and hang them on a rack or on the handle of a brush across some chairs. The puddings would be shared between the neighbours with a few slices of the pig steak, and of course, they'd do the same for you when it was their turn to kill the pig. She loved it when the neighbours gathered like this and life was brightened by chat and banter. They all looked forward to the harvest round up too, when they gathered, the men to help with the cutting of the barley, oats and hay, and the women to bake and cook. Those were happy times, and it was grand to see Sonny racing around with the other children and getting rides on top of the hay ricks back to the barns. There would be music, dancing and merrymaking afterwards and the priests rarely bothered them, though someone would always keep a lookout. They had all surely been awestruck that evening in Maguire's big kitchen when Jimmy Maguire brought out the first gramophone most of them had ever seen. The record he played was of John McCormack singing the *Snowy Breasted Pearl*.

As time went on, there were fewer to help with the harvest and the young ones continued to leave. Sure it was only to be expected that they wanted more social life and money, and it was in the city that they'd get that. Fear would clutch at her throat then as she looked at her little boy; would he want to leave too?

What a wonderful day it was when Rosy and her husband Mark, with their little girl Rachel, came all the way from New York to see her in Doonbeg. She and Rebecca had always written to her at Christmas enclosing a few dollars, but now Rosy was touring Ireland by motorcar and coming to visit her. The excitement of it: Peadar put a fresh coat of whitewash on the house and sheds, and she bought six matching cups and saucers in Kilrush market to replace their cracked ones. She still had the table cloth she'd brought home from New York and Annie baked some soda bread and an apple tart for her. Well, it was a beautiful sunny day, the yard all swept clean with the manure tucked behind one of the sheds. Sonny, who was six then, must have got caught up in the excitement, never complaining about his new shoes, though she knew that they hurt him. It was his friend Charlie who dashed across the fields to tell her that they were on their way, having left their motor car surrounded by curious neighbours at the entrance to the boreen.

Her little Rosy was a grown woman and so beautiful; she cried on seeing her and Rosy hugged her tight. She couldn't remember much about Mark but Rachel was a lovely dark eyed child, and so pretty in her blue dress, pleated from below her little hips, with white ankle socks and strapped red shoes of patent leather. It was lovely to see her delight in the two pet lambs, begging Sonny to let her feed them, and after he brought her out to the shed to show her the new litter of five kittens, they didn't see her until it was time to go. They left promising to visit again, leaving her with queer feelings of loneliness.

Peadar did a bit of inshore fishing, and he and the other fishermen were always railing against the government for failing to develop the industry. "Look at Grimsby on the east coast of England," he'd say "Why wouldn't they invest in harbours like that here and provide the jobs our local boys could do with." It was following a fishing trip in November that he caught the cold that would develop into pneumonia. It was the day after Christmas when she knew that he was going to die: Wren's Day. A grey mist hugged the house and yard that morning, and the early half-light barely struggled through the clouds. The wind had whirled some loose fencing across the cobbled yard during the night, but had died down, and she gave in to Sonny's pleas to be allowed go out with his friends a-hunting the wren. She helped him blacken his face with boot polish and dressed him up in some old skirt of hers, glad to see him so excited.

Afterwards kneeling on the hearth to stir the embers into fire, she noticed the scattered sparks glancing off Peadar's old boots as he stood leaning against the table. His face, lined and tired, took light from the new fire but this just emphasized the pallid yellowish tinge of his skin and his rheumy bloodshot eyes. She was surprised when he leant down as she knelt back on her heels and stroked her loose grey hair, something he'd never done before. "You're not well," she told him, "you need to get into bed," and his passive acceptance frightened her even more than his pallor. She ran across to Annie's house knowing that Michael had a bicycle. Dr O'Brien drove him into Kilrush hospital in his motor car, but he was dead within three days.

She gazed at the familiar body, washed and laid out by the neighbouring women. There were candles at his feet and in the windows. The neighbours filed in quietly, the women fingering their rosary beads and the men clutching their caps in their hands. The low whisperings of the praying women seemed fretful, and she was aware of skitterings in the thatch. She wondered vaguely if there were rats up there and was embarrassed by the stench from the chamber pot under the bed that she'd forgotten to empty His face was so peaceful; how she could ever have taken all that good nature and good humour for granted. She suddenly had a surge of panic; who was going to look after the farm, plough and sow, raise the cattle and pigs. Peadar had taken care of all that, and she had never wanted to know much about it; she had Sonny to look after. She must have said something because the neighbours looked at her strangely. Everything from then on was hazy, and she had little memory of the wake or funeral that followed. The neighbours too had been shocked by the suddenness of his death, and though there was drink and food, and the clay pipes filled with tobacco were handed round, there was little conversation and no music. They all of them felt for her and her orphaned boy.

With Peadar gone she had to rely on the help of neighbours to carry out the work of the farm, and it was with their help that she got by the years that followed. They would carry her milk to the creamery and help out with the harvest, or cutting the turf, and potato picking. She'd gradually given up the milking and began to keep dry stock which meant a lot less labour. The neighbours would buy calves for her to fatten before being sold at the fair and it meant that Sonny didn't have to get up early to help with the milking before school. She knew from the teacher that he was doing well at school, and she was proud of the fact that he could already read and write, so she did not want to tire him out with too much work.

When the Second World War broke out, droves of the young men in West Clare signed up with the British Army. They wanted to escape the unemployment and like all young men were out for a bit of adventure. She was surely glad that by the time Sonny left school, the war had come to an end. Sure in those times the life blood of the country was draining away as more and more young people emigrated to find work, and she lived in constant dread of Sonny leaving her. By the time he was fourteen or fifteen the neighbours were always at her to make him take on the work of the farm, but he was unwilling, telling her he hated farm work, and spoke of looking for factory work in England where some of his school friends had already gone. Fearful of his leaving, she knew that she gave in to him too easily, and gradually the land that Peadar had kept in such good order began to return to its scrubby wild state.

A Clarewoman's Journey

The drip, drip of water woke her; it was still only half-light. She heard rather than saw the raindrops plopping close to the back wall of the bedroom where she knew the roof was letting in. She'd asked Sonny to fix it a few times now, but like everything else, he'd say he would but didn't do anything about it. Billy, good soul that he was, offered to fix it for her but she was ashamed with a strapping son of her own, so just told him that Sonny was planning to get round to it when he had a minute. She peered out at the grey spears of falling rain turning the dung to a mucky liquid that pooled around the yard; there were too many of these sodden grey days.

She sighed then at the wearisome round of her life; up by six to boil the yellow meal and potatoes for the pigs and hens, while she made her way time and again to the well carrying water for the tea and the cooking. Wasn't it grand in New York with the water on tap, but sure she was thankful to have the river so near for the washing and the cleaning. Then there was the baking and cooking, keeping the fire going and making sure that Sonny was clean and had his porridge before school. By the time evening came and she threw herself down on a bit of old newspaper on the hard floor to say the rosary, she was half dead with the tiredness. She used often feel trapped as she looked up at the picture of the Sacred Heart, only the lower half of which was lit by the little oil lamp.

"Trying to ridge that oul field would break your back," Sonny complained when the time came round for planting the potato seed, and though she helped with the harvesting, he was bitter about that too. "Why can't we buy the few potatoes we need from Michael Ryan," he'd asked, "they always have extra to sell." She was angry then and for once gave him a piece of her mind: "You are a lazy, good-for-nothing and 'tis a crying

shame that your father isn't here to beat some sense into you. Do you think I'm made of money?"

"Don't you get money every month from Uncle Paddy
over in Boston." It was a shock to her to find that he
was cute enough to notice the monthly money order
she received faithfully from Peadar's brother since his
death. Like many of her neighbours she relied on those
dollars to keep her and Sonny in tea, sugar and bread,
but unlike many of them, she knew how hard earned
this money was. Without fail, every year, she'd send
Paddy a letter at Christmas and St Patrick's Day, when
she'd put some dried shamrock in with it. She never let
on to Sonny about the money she'd brought home
from New York before he was born. It was nearly
twenty years ago now, and she hadn't checked for a
while, but she knew it would still be in the rubber
pouch she'd made. She had tucked it inside her mattress which she'd carefully sewn up again. Even Peadar
had not known about it, and nobody was ever allowed
into the room above the fireplace where she slept. Now
she hardly even let on to herself that she had it; it was
her protection against eviction and the workhouse.
They told her that the workhouse wasn't there anymore
but wasn't the county home just another name for the
workhouse?

CHAPTER 19

Eilin Lets Go …

I found it hard to shake off the misery I felt, following my visit to the caravan site just south of Kilkee. The local parish priest was consulted by the police, who had received notification via a social service department in England about a family moving there and there being concerns about the welfare of the children. There wasn't enough evidence to take any action, but they were worried for their safety. As always in such cases, it was with real trepidation that I visited the family. The children were of school age, so my approach was based on the need to ensure that arrangements were in place for them to start school.

The dark young man who answered my knock had deeply indented lines of anger around his mouth and eyes. He did not greet me but asked abruptly what I wanted. I was clear with him that we had been notified by the authorities about concerns around the children's safety and would need to visit regularly. I was frightened by the surge of rage that suffused his face. His wife or partner came out to stand beside him, and she put her hand on his arm which seemed to act as a check. She was a skeletally thin woman with a drawn, androgynous face and deep shadows under both eyes. I had never before experienced such a palpable wall of hostility and rage. I asked if I could see the children and was reluctantly allowed to enter. The two little girls, about eight and nine, were quiet and wary and always

155

glanced at their parents before answering my simple questions in monosyllables.

During subsequent visits, they were more welcoming and friendly. They tried to convince me that they had been victims of harassment and prejudice on the part of the English police. They spoke of their preference for living in Ireland and of how much they liked Irish people. If anything I became even more uneasy. I liaised with the school but was painfully aware of the inadequacy of any protective environment afforded by my visits and the school's watchful concern. Living with such unease was to become familiar over the course of my professional life, but this first experience, without the support of professional colleagues, was a source of acute anxiety.

When Rosy and Mark wrote to tell Eilin that they planned to visit her in the early 1950s, she wanted to put them off but didn't know how. In any case, they were already on their way by the time she got the letter. She didn't have the energy to do much. She asked Sonny to clean the house and yard, maybe put on a coat of whitewash. While he said he'd get around to it, she watched the days go by with nothing done, until the day before they were due when he made a half-hearted attempt to sweep up the yard. She told Annie about the visit when she called in with some messages, and bless her didn't she come down and clean the whole house so that she wouldn't be ashamed. She no longer had the nice table cloth, but at least the table was clean, and Annie brought her down some fresh brown bread that morning. It was nice to see Rosy, but the visit was a pity because you'd know that they were a bit shocked at seeing the place so run down. Sonny didn't come near the house, and when Rosy asked for him, she just said that he had to go to the fishing. When they left there was an envelope with £20 on the table, and she cried, it wasn't money she needed then.

She knew that she was losing Sonny. Even if he didn't go to England or America, he didn't want to be at home with her. Every evening he was off with some of the local boys. He'd say he was going to a hurling match or they were playing a game themselves, but she knew they often cycled into Kilrush and God only knows what they'd get up to there. Then didn't he spend any night he wasn't out, up at the O'Brien's watching the television, and this was changing all the old ways. The priests used to be dead against it at first, but the people didn't care and everyone watched Gay Byrne and the *Late Late Show*, where people weren't shy of saying just what they thought.

"Bedad those boyos are not afraid of upsetting the powers that be." She was in the hardware shop in Kilrush when she heard Garda Molloy and the shop owner discussing the *Seven Days* programme which had been on the night before. She knew that this was a programme determined to root out the truth of things, and it had a lot of influence. It would take on the politicians, priests and even the bishops. Then there was the soap opera about an Irish country family, *The Riordans;* Sonny would tell her what they got up to every week, and she used to look forward to hearing about them. The young ones seemed to be a lot freer and were less fearful of what the church thought. They went their own way too, paying little attention to the wishes of their parents, and her Sonny was no different.

He wanted to be free to live his own life, and she knew that he had no interest in farming, but God forgive her, she couldn't let him go. Bad cess to all them young ones coming home from London and New York with money in their pockets and putting ideas into his head. She knew that her efforts to reach him were no use. She used to tell him about how hard people had to work to earn money in those places and how lonely they could be. Wasn't he lucky to have a place of his own and no-one bossing him around? She felt helpless as he became more withdrawn and many was the night she'd cry herself to sleep as she yearned for a return of that love they had in his childhood. She thought long-ingly of those times, when as a child he'd put his little hand into hers if the dog barked too loudly or there was a big herd of cows on the boreen. That trust was surely slipping away from her as the years went on, and he drifted aimlessly through his days. Rising late in the morning he did little work around the farm, and the house gradually began to fall around their ears.

"Sonny is a nice enough creature but sure he's useless, what is poor Eilin going to do?" Mary Mc Grath didn't notice her slipping into the shop and had reddened on turning to find her there. Oh, she raged inwardly at the neighbours, aware of their contempt for Sonny, but mostly at her own helplessness. Liam O'Brien had sure-ly been exasperated when they'd gathered to help Sonny harvest their hay, and stacked it all up into neat ricks before the weather broke. Liam warned him to get these tied down that night because of the storm that was threatening, but Sonny hadn't bothered. Sure enough, there was a gale that night and all the hay they'd saved and stacked, was blown away all over the place. Oh Liam was furious, and you couldn't blame him, but poor Sonny just stood there with his head bowed muttering that he had been too tired. By then she didn't care too much herself about any of it, noth-ing seemed that important anymore.

I knew that my sympathies had shifted as Eilin's tale unfolded. Her harsh and often lonely life was at least that ... her life. Was there not a touch of the Miss Havisham about that begrimed old lady? I became increasingly conscious of the shadowy man flitting in and out of that run down cottage over the course of my visits. I thought it unlikely now that he would ever emerge from the twilight world where Eilin's desperate need and his own lack of courage kept him trapped. Perhaps it wasn't a want of courage but a generous, despairing empathy for her loneliness. If so, the truth of Yeats's line "too long a sacrifice makes a stone of the heart" must surely apply. Eilin's physical and emotional dependency offered no support for the fragile growth of a separate identity. Indeed, the pressures and expectations arising from this must have forged unbreakable emotional fetters for a shy young man.

My sympathies were to veer back again not long after when I walked up and down the ward in Kilrush hospital to which I'd been directed. I had been in Dublin for the weekend and didn't hear of Eilin's admission the previous Friday until I returned on the Monday morning. Seriously ill with pneumonia, she had been delirious when the neighbours called the ambulance. Now, in a curious reprisal of our first introduction, I looked in vain for the familiar figure. Eventually, one of the nurses brought me over to a tiny, faded but very clean, wispy creature, and it took me some time to recognise my grimy feisty friend in this new disguise. The old lady looked at me unseeingly as I took her hand and soon her eyelids closed over. She died that night, which wasn't uncommon, the nurse said, when patients were washed clean of years of grime. Her quiet, modest ending gave no clue to the colourful eventful life she had revealed to me over the previous months.

I sighed, thinking of my own more subtle emotional bondage. Comfort in being employed and cherished by the church should be in my DNA. My family was littered with priests, nuns, missionaries and even bishops. I myself spent two years preparing for the life of a missionary nun and had relished the silence, physical discipline and pursuit of the spiritual. Truth to tell, part of it was probably the freedom from personal responsibility to chart the course of my own life, a scary prospect for an unconfident seventeen-year-old. I'd left the convent but now, professionally embraced by the church I struggled to understand why I felt ever so slightly yet persistently compromised. I was surrounded by, and worked with, people of faith whom I admired and was comfortable with, and was well able to resist pressure if I didn't agree with it.

I had a fierce allegiance to the spiritual legacy inherited via the church – the aspiration to disinterested love at the heart of the Christian message and the liturgical support to make this real in day-to-day life. This sat uncomfortably alongside anger against an all-male power structure that often seemed at odds with that message and more focused on sustaining itself than delivering it. Though comfortable within the admirably tolerant ambience of a growing secular culture, I found it a woefully inadequate response to any deeper yearnings.

Was it the persistence of these feelings, the prolonged period of dark heavy cloud and relentless rain that summer, the prospect of facing into another winter alone over the empty shoe shop in Kilrush square, or the image of Sonny trapped down that narrow boreen in Doonbeg that decided me to move to Dublin, and set up house with my New York boyfriend?

Och well …

Epilogue

Eilin's story is fictional but informed by the glimpse I had into the intriguing lives of an old lady and her son whom I got to know as a social worker in West Clare. The trajectory of this woman's life, from her birth in a cabin on the remote Loophead peninsula to the crowded streets of New York, aged barely seventeen, and back again to rural life in West Clare in her thirties, was dramatic. It encompassed enormous personal, cultural and historical change. Her simple upbringing can hardly have equipped her for domestic service with the prosperous and sophisticated of New York, nor for her immersion in the multi-layered, cosmopolitan life of the city. Dramatic too were the historical events encompassed within the span of her life ... the First and Second World Wars, the 1916 Easter Rising and Ireland's war of independence, as well as the civil war that followed. All of these will have impacted on her alongside local events and changes, both in New York and in Clare. It is not hard to imagine the pain and loneliness that must have accompanied the adjustments called for. More unexpected perhaps are the likely joys and freedoms of such a journey. Her return to a terribly changed Ireland, still characterised by poverty, unemployment and emigration, must have had a dampening effect on the optimism which brought her back home in the mid-Twenties.

While my encounters with this old lady sparked an interest in trying to imagine what was entailed in such a life, I need to be very clear that Eilin's story is not hers. Though I gave her some of the trappings of this woman's experience, the character, behaviour and motivations of Eilin are purely fictional, as are those of the other characters involved. The rest of the story was based on historical research into the period covered by her life in West Clare and New York, both local and general. Her part in the historical events described is also fictional, as are the parts played by the other characters. I have tried to be true to historical record, by placing them in situations and amongst people who either did exist or might have done. The excerpts from my own life are based on personal experience as a social worker in West Clare at that time. The names of persons referred to have been changed to protect privacy.

When I first got to know this woman she lived with her son in conditions as described in Eilin's story. She was born and raised near the spectacular Bridges of Ross on the northern shore of the Loophead peninsula. An elderly neighbour whom I interviewed thought that her family, and another family of the same name in the neighbourhood, were likely to have been evicted from Cross, a village and townland further in towards Kilkee and presumably with better land. She stated that a lot of people were evicted from there, back in the 19th century.

It was known that this woman went to New York and into service, and indeed had been preceded there by two older girls who were very likely cousins as well as close neighbours of the family. This latter family was a large one and known for its intelligence and musicality, and a further member of this family reputedly married a man from Doonbeg. It would seem likely that she was instrumental in suggesting the match with a local farmer when this was being discussed with the matchmaker in the area. He was, by all accounts, a good farmer with a well-maintained farm and home. In any event, she returned to marry into this farm and in 1930 her son was born. She was then forty years of age. All reports from neighbours who knew the family indicate that she probably spoiled the son, made a *"peata"* out of him and that this, to a large extent, explained his laziness as a farmer, and his failure to prevent the house falling down about them.

They were described as lovely people and very intelligent by all, who knew and spoke of them. "You could not have better neighbours," asserted a close friend and neighbour. "If ever any help was needed for lambing, or with a sick animal or anything, you could rely on the son who would stay with you twenty-four hours if need be; yet you couldn't get him to accept help for himself and the mother."

"Many's the time," he added, "when myself and other neighbours offered to fix up the house for them but they wouldn't accept. He was good to others but no good to himself." Others, more abrasively, described him as nice but useless. They were said to be very proud and hated the thought of charity. Even when the local river beside their house flooded their home as it was wont to do fairly frequently, being a tidal river, they would not come up to stay with the neighbours but raised themselves off the floor onto the table until it subsided. So as the years went on, the house got more and more dilapidated, yet they regularly got the newspapers, would discuss politics very intelligently, and were, folk said, great talkers.

The other surprising thing was that the home and farm the old lady had married into was described as one of the best and most attractive in the area. It was at that time very well-maintained, beautifully thatched and kept freshly whitewashed. There was a row of well-built outhouses running at right angles to the main cottage and a robust cobbled yard. None of this was apparent in the dereliction within which I first encountered her in 1974. When the

163

Land Commission was replacing the old thatched homes with new stone houses with running water and electricity, she refused to budge and remained without any of these amenities right up to when I knew her at the age of eighty-five.

It is difficult to understand, how someone who had known good standards of domestic culture from her time in New York, and who would, presumably, have learnt how to care for a home, could let herself drift into such a state of decline. Indeed, she and her son were clearly in close and friendly contact with their neighbours, and people were well disposed toward them. The people all around were able to take advantage of the new opportunities and provisions opening up during the first half of the 20th century. They would have seen their neighbours availing of improved housing provision, and the installation of electricity, running water and sanitation, yet they themselves failed to do so.

It is, I suppose, likely that their inclinations were more cerebral than practical and that they were indifferent to the material conditions in which they lived. If so, the awfulness of the conditions, and the extent of their indifference would seem almost pathological. It could well be that a level of deep undiagnosed depression lay behind the apathy, and the finding of a substantial sum of money hidden away in the house after the old lady's death suggests that what was known as the "Famine mentality", whereby people held on to sums of money as a talisman against the threat of eviction or hunger, also played a part.

I learned in the course of my research that the family she had worked for in New York visited her in Doonbeg on two occasions. Even more astonishingly, her son made two visits to New York after her death and went on to marry the daughter of this family who returned with him to West Clare. She was rumoured to have sons by a previous marriage, and may have had fairly bohemian inclinations which allowed her to sustain his way of life for the years she did. She was also described by neighbours as being a lovely person, and they told of her arriving into the local shop one morning, following a night of flooding. The water had spread all round their mobile home, which was lodged on the family land beside the old derelict cottage, but she was delighted, saying that she " had gone to bed with the moon and woken up in a lake."

However, it must have got too much for her because she eventually returned to America. According to a neighbour, the last straw was when the old lady's son refused to connect them up to the electricity supply, which would have only entailed connecting a cable across a couple of fields. Nevertheless, they remained married, and the headstone erected in Doonbeg cemetery in memory of this man and his parents was erected by his wife.

Acknowledgements

I am indebted to archival resources such as the National Libraries of Scotland and Ireland and Clare Social Studies Centre. Thanks are due to the many friends and contacts in west Clare who generously gave of time and knowledge in order to help me fill in the background to *A Clarewoman's Journey*. You know who you are: thank you.

I also owe a debt of gratitude to the family members, friends and strangers who helped to bring this project to fruition. Foremost are the staff of the superb Clare Social Studies Centre who were hugely helpful. I am particularly indebted to librarian Peter Beirne whose generosity in reading my typescript prior to publication and providing useful feedback was very much appreciated. Thanks are also due to the many friends who offered support – in particular Kathleen Loughnane, Jamie Gilchrist, Orna Gilchrist, Moya Cannon, Katherine Dickie, Margaret Coffey, Mairin Eydmann, Sylvia O'Neill and Maureen Kinnell, all of whom took the trouble to read the early awkward drafts and provide such helpful comment.

I am indebted to the three poets quoted in the text; Michael Coady, whose poem *Time's Kiss* is contained in the collection *All Souls* published by The Gallery Press in 1997, Moya Cannon for her poem *Thirst in the Burren* from her 2000 collection *Oar*, also published by the Gallery Press, and the late Seamas Heaney, whose poem *Postscript* is to be found in *New Selected Poems 1988-2013* published by Faber & Faber Ltd.

A huge thank you to Edinburgh graphic designer, Laura Donnelly for her excellent cover design. Finally and most importantly I need to thank my husband Jim, who undertook the laborious and thankless task of proofreading the final draft as well as offering constructive feedback and unfailing support.

55886599R00092

Made in the USA
Charleston, SC
11 May 2016